"Would you ... to... ...?"

Ronan asked Deirdre.

Yes, I mind! But she felt trapped by the little voice inside that reminded her it would be rude to refuse. Ronan was looking at her, his eyes the color of tiger-eye topaz alive with interest. "All right," Deirdre said before she could think too much more about it.

Ronan nodded. "I'll come by tomorrow, then." He took her hand in his to say goodbye.

Driving home a few minutes later, Deirdre was a mass of churning anxiety. Why was she letting him into her home? She didn't want to look at a man, let alone think about one.

Without warning, the memory of his big hand taking hers returned. The man radiated warmth. And she hadn't been warm in a very long time....

Dear Reader,

Happy Valentine's Day! And what better way to celebrate Cupid's reign than by reading six brand-new Desire novels...?

Putting us in the mood for sensuous love is this February's MAN OF THE MONTH, with wonderful Dixie Browning offering us the final title in her THE LAWLESS HEIRS miniseries in *A Knight in Rusty Armor.* This alpha-male hero knows just what to do when faced with a sultry damsel in distress!

Continue to follow the popular Fortune family's romances in the Desire series FORTUNE'S CHILDREN: THE BRIDES. The newest installment, *Society Bride* by Elizabeth Bevarly, features a spirited debutante who runs away from a business-deal marriage...into the arms of the rugged rancher of her dreams.

Ever-talented Anne Marie Winston delivers the second story in her BUTLER COUNTY BRIDES, with a single mom opening her home and heart to a seductive acquaintance, in *Dedicated to Deirdre.* Then a modern-day cowboy renounces his footloose ways for love in *The Outlaw Jesse James,* the final title in Cindy Gerard's OUTLAW HEARTS miniseries; while a child's heartwarming wish for a father is granted in Raye Morgan's *Secret Dad.* And with *Little Miss Innocent?* Lori Foster proves that opposites *do* attract.

This Valentine's Day, Silhouette Desire's little red books sizzle with compelling romance and make the perfect gift for the contemporary woman—you! So treat yourself to all six!

Enjoy!

Joan Marlow Golan
Senior Editor, Silhouette Desire

Please address questions and book requests to:
Silhouette Reader Service
U.S.: 3010 Walden Ave., P.O. Box 1325, Buffalo, NY 14269
Canadian: P.O. Box 609, Fort Erie, Ont. L2A 5X3

DEDICATED TO DEIRDRE
ANNE MARIE WINSTON

SILHOUETTE *Desire*®

Published by Silhouette Books

America's Publisher of Contemporary Romance

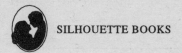

SILHOUETTE BOOKS

ISBN 0-373-76197-X

DEDICATED TO DEIRDRE

This edition published by arrangement with Harlequin Books S.A.

® and TM are trademarks of Harlequin Books S.A., used under license. Trademarks indicated with ® are registered in the United States Patent and Trademark Office, the Canadian Trade Marks Office and in other countries.

Printed in U.S.A.

ANNE MARIE WINSTON

has believed in happy endings all her life. Having the opportunity to share them with her readers gives her great joy. Anne Marie enjoys figure skating and working in the gardens of her south-central Pennsylvania home.

For Nora
Who has great taste in shoes, champagne
and pals (!)
And who excels at midnight readings.

One

"Lee! Don't pull—"

Too late. Deirdre Patten's oldest son used every ounce of his wiry five-year-old strength to tug a box of sugared cereal from the very bottom of an enormous stack of the breakfast foods in the grocery store. With an experienced eye born of many brushes with disaster, she instantly calculated that she was too far away to grab her son. Her heart lurched as the entire stack tilted and began to slide slowly forward. Visions of the grievous injury a huge stack of boxes could do to a little boy flashed across her mind as she dashed forward, and in the same instant, the entire array of cereal boxes crashed to the floor right in front of her.

"Lee! Honey, where are you?" Frantically she kicked aside boxes, then dropped to her knees looking for a little arm or leg beneath the avalanche. "Lee? *Lee!*"

"Hi, Mommy!"

Her heart began to beat again when she heard the chirpy little voice. She paused in the middle of her frantic shoveling and looked around. On the other side of the aisle, Lee was waving to her. He stood beside a stranger, a man with dark chestnut hair, a man who had Lee's wrist in a firm grasp.

"Baby, are you all right?" She leaped over the boxes and knelt beside her son, running her hands over him. Nothing looked broken. "How many times have I told you—"

"The man saved me, Mom." Lee was pointing up, and she realized the man who had released her son's wrist must have pulled him out of the way of the boxes.

She sat back on her heels with a weary smile. "Thank you so much. This one and his little brother keep me…on my…toes." Her voice drained away to nothing as she recognized the man looking down at her.

"Hello…Mrs. Patten, I believe?"

The voice was the same, deep and slightly rough, with a lazy drawl to the words that made a woman's toes curl. She'd noticed that the night of the office Christmas party in Baltimore, Maryland, three years ago even though she'd been so upset with her husband she could barely see straight.

Slowly she got to her feet, keeping her hands on her son's shoulders in front of her. "Hello."

He extended a large, tanned hand. "Ronan Sullivan. We've met before."

She flushed, a nod her only acknowledgment as she reached out to shake his hand. "Deirdre is my first name, but my friends call me Dee. This is Lee and my other son, in the cart, is Tommy." She barely touched his fingers before drawing back quickly. His hand was warm and firm, and the brief moment when her hand was in his produced an unsettling instant of awareness that she forced herself to ignore. "Thank you for your quick thinking. Lee could have been badly hurt."

"You're welcome. No problem." He grazed his knuckles across the top of Lee's closely shaved head of black fuzz. "I saw it coming, so I was ready for a quick rescue."

"Ah, well, thank you again." She cast a glance at her cart to make sure Tommy hadn't strayed from his seat in the front. A store employee had come running and was restacking the boxes.

"You're welcome again." He hesitated for a bare instant. "Is your husband still with Bethlehem Steel?"

"Yes," she said, though why he would mention her husband after the last time they'd met was beyond her. She'd hoped that perhaps he'd forgotten some of the more humiliating details of that evening.

"Long commute from out here. Do you live in the area?"

She hesitated, then decided there was no reason to keep her situation a secret. Sooner or later she had to begin to tell people. "I'm divorced now. I have a farm halfway between Butler and Frizzelburg."

His eyes warmed, though he didn't smile. "My grandparents had a farm down in Virginia. Do you work it?"

She shook her head. "I lease most of the land to the man who has the place next to ours. I have a small business that keeps me pretty busy."

"What do you do?"

She twisted her fingers together, then caught herself and flattened her palms against her sides. "It's nothing, really. I design and make a line of doll clothes."

"Hmm."

She couldn't tell what that meant, but she felt defensiveness rising around her like a growing field of corn. "It allows me to make enough to live on and still be home with the boys."

"That's important."

"It is to me." She glanced over at Tommy, who was showing signs of restlessness, a prelude, she knew, to a leap from the cart. "Well, I must be going. It was nice to see you again." A blatant lie. Seeing Ronan Sullivan stirred up all kinds of memories of her old life, memories she was determined to forget.

"Before you go," he said. "Would you know of anyone with a place to rent in the area? I'm looking for—"

"Mom!" Lee clutched at her hand. "Maybe he's the one! Ask him."

"No." She loved her sons but there were times when she thought seriously of locking them away for a day or ten. "I'm sure Mr.—"

"Ronan," he reminded her.

"Ronan," she repeated dutifully, "wouldn't be interested in the apartment."

"What apartment?" He was looking at her for an answer, eyes the color of tigereye topaz suddenly alive with interest.

"It's nothing great," she said quickly. "I'm looking for a tenant to rent the apartment over the stable. It's very small and extremely rustic. I'm sure it wouldn't suit you."

"You never know. Would you mind if I looked at it?"

Yes, I mind! But she felt trapped by the little voice inside—a little voice that sounded strangely like her mother's—that reminded her that it would be rude to refuse.

Really, there was no reason for her to worry. She'd envisioned renting to a woman, but why should a man be any different? A civilized man. He's not Nelson, she told herself firmly. One bad apple doesn't spoil the whole barrel. Making up her mind, she said, "All right," before she could think too much more about it. "But don't expect too much. It's primitive."

He nodded. "I'd still like to look at it. Is tomorrow convenient?"

Tomorrow! "Tomorrow would be fine. Around eleven?" Maybe he would be working; she could always say evenings didn't suit, just stall until—

"Eleven it is."

Driving home through the quiet Butler County countryside a few minutes later, she was a mass of churning anxiety inside. Why was she letting him look at the apartment? She didn't want a man hanging around her home, good apples in the barrel or not. She didn't want to talk with a man, didn't want to look at a man, didn't even want to think about one. She had a few exceptions—her brothers, her friend Frannie's husband, but she had grown up with Jack so he didn't really count...but other than that, she deliberately avoided even making eye contact with the opposite sex. The thought of so much as a casual date left a very bad taste in her mouth.

She'd planned to fix up the apartment, rent it to a career woman who wouldn't be home much. Still, maybe a male tenant wouldn't be such a bad thing. She wouldn't have to see much of him, would hardly know he was there.

Without warning, the memory of his big hand taking hers returned. The man felt like a big heater, radiating warmth. And she hadn't been warm in a very long time.

It was perfect, Ronan thought as his white pickup truck crested the hill on the rutted lane that led to Deirdre Patten's place. A perfect place to write. Not a reporter or a determined fan in sight, and none likely to find him easily.

And to make it even better, he had his research right under his nose. Fields on his right, forest on his left. The fields sloped gently down to a wide, flat valley through which a little stream meandered. A stone farmhouse—an old stone farmhouse, from the look of it—was surrounded by a neat square of yard, and across the gravel driveway, an equally ancient barn loomed. Beside the barn was what looked like a chicken house, a pig sty and finally a smaller, and much newer, stable painted a traditional barn red with white crossbars. Green fields, interspersed with stands of tall trees and fencerows overgrown with climbing vines, spread out in every direction.

It looked like a picture on a postcard titled, "America, Circa 1950." And it was right off the highway, though no one would ever guess it was there.

Taking his foot off the brake, he let the truck coast down the lane, trying in vain to avoid the worst ruts. He'd probably have to have the wheels aligned every couple of months if he stayed here.

Halfway down the lane, he slammed on the brakes abruptly. The wheels skidded in the loose stone, then caught and held as he pumped the pedal. What the hell—?

Dead smack in the middle of the lane were the two little Patten boys, Lee of the cereal box slide and his little brother—had Deirdre said his name was Tommy? They were hunched over something on the ground, something that made a heck of a lot of dust. One had a handful of leaves he was cautiously stuffing into whatever it was. They were so absorbed in what they were doing that neither one of them even heard the truck.

He considered blowing the horn, but he didn't want to scare the little fellas, so he opened his door and swung out of the truck, intending to call to them to move out of the road.

That's when he saw the flames.

"Hey!" That wasn't dust; it was fire! He didn't have much experience with kids, but he knew nobody in their right mind would allow boys this small to mess around with fire.

As he started forward, the oldest child looked up. A broad smile split his face and he hollered, "Hi-ya, Mr. Sullivan, it works! Come see our fire!"

Since he planned on doing exactly that, he walked up and hunkered down beside the smaller boy. The flames were still a tiny blaze, hungrily licking at the leaves. "What are you doing?"

Tommy held up a magnifying glass. "On TV Yogi an' Boo-Boo started a fire wif a mag-i, man-i—"

"Magnifying glass," supplied his brother. "And so did we!"

"Umm, that's interesting." Ronan took the magnifying glass and pretended to examine it while he eyed the little blaze. "But you don't want that fire to get very big."

"No," agreed the littlest boy. He stood and pulled something out of one pocket of the sturdy, very grubby jeans he wore. "We're gonna put it out."

Glancing down at the small hand thrust under his nose, Ronan couldn't help but grin. The little guy had a yellow plastic water pistol, primed with enough water to douse a match—maybe. "Good idea," he told the child solemnly, pressing his lips together to prevent the chuckle that was trying to escape. "But I know another way to put out a small fire like this. Want me to show you?"

"Okay!" Both little boys stepped back as he stood.

"Fire needs air to breathe, just like you do," he explained. "I'm going to step on it, keep it from getting any air, until it dies."

"Can we help?"

"Sure." Anything to get that fire out before it realized how much prime fuel surrounded it. "One, two, three, stomp!" And as he did, he slipped the magnifying glass into his pocket. Where in the heck was their mother, and what was she thinking, to be letting them try a dangerous stunt like this?

It didn't take much convincing to get the boys interested in a ride in the truck—another issue he'd mention to their mother. He boosted them in and drove on down the lane to the house, parking in the graveled area next to the old barn. As he lifted each child from the truck, a battered green Bronco came jouncing across the pasture farthest from him. As it neared, he saw Deirdre was driving. She looked scared and upset—until she saw the children. Then her expression changed to pure fury.

She was out of the Bronco almost before it slid to a stop. "Where were you?" she demanded. "I specifically told you to stay in the yard." Her pretty, heart-shaped face was stern, and she tapped her foot as she waited for an answer.

Ronan was fascinated. He'd thought the phrase, "Vibrated with anger," was a figurative description until now.

"But the yawd burns," Tommy offered.

"Yeah, we didn't want to start a *big* fire," said Lee.

"A fire?" Her green eyes grew round. "Where did you get matches? What did you set fire to? Is it still burning?"

Ronan cleared his throat as he reached into his pocket, offering her the magnifying lens. "The intrepid scouts here didn't need matches. I helped them put it out."

"You're kidding." She took the item from him as if it might bite. "You actually started a fire with this?" she said to the boys.

"Yep!" Tommy, less experienced at reading his mother's ire, swelled with pride.

She didn't miss a beat. "And is it okay to play with fire?"

Both children visibly sagged. Small voices muttered, "No."

"That's right," she said. "And what's the rule about fire?"

"There has to be a grown-up with us." The older boy looked chastened—but not exactly sorry.

"And what happens when you don't follow the rules?"

As one, two little faces fell, and they turned toward the house. "Go to our rooms," they said in mournful unison.

"I'll let you know when you can come out," she called after them. Then she turned to Ronan. "Mr. Sullivan, I don't know what to say, except thank you again." She sighed, looking at the magnifying glass and shaking her head. "They can find things to get into that I've never even thought of."

He couldn't suppress his grin any longer. "They were pretty proud of that trick."

She shuddered. "Thank God you came along when you did. I went the other way to look for them because that creek is like a magnet. I was sure they were down there." She slipped the lens into her own pocket. "You know, if you decide to stay here, you'll have to put up with them."

He chuckled. "They aren't so bad. Just lively."

"You can say that again." She shook her head in exasperation and blew out a breath as she shoved stray black curls out of her peripheral vision. Pointing to the stable as she began to walk, she indicated that he should follow her. "I'm sure you'll think twice about this apartment when you see it. I've been planning to fix it up, but I just haven't gotten around to it yet. As I said, it needs a lot of work."

"I don't mind work," he said mildly.

"And Butler County isn't exactly a hotbed of social events. You'll have to drive back into Baltimore for any kind of nightlife."

"Definitely not high on my list." The thought of social events led like an electrical current through a chain of thought that halted at the first time he'd ever met this woman. As he followed her into the barn and up a flight of stairs, he could almost see her sitting in a pool of candlelight, a strained, obviously false smile pasted on her pretty face.

The social event had been the annual Christmas party for the office employees of Bethlehem Steel. His cousin Arden, being between boyfriends, had invited him. He hadn't any plans, so he'd agreed to go. They were seated at dinner by name cards, eight to a table. He and Arden had been paired with one of the company vice presidents and his wife, the vice president's executive secretary and her husband, and Deirdre and Nelson Patten, who was another top executive.

Drink had flowed freely during dinner, too freely, and Patten had gotten slurring and stupid, well before the end of the meal. His wife had sat in embarrassed silence, eyes on her plate unless someone spoke directly to her.

He'd been struck by her unusual beauty, unable to keep his eyes off her—and the first time she'd risen to visit the ladies' room, he'd realized that she was heavily pregnant. He'd never thought pregnant women were particularly sexy, but his body seemed to forget that when he looked at Deirdre Patten.

Even obviously unhappy, she was strikingly pretty, with soft roses blooming under the fair skin along her high cheekbones and big, long-lashed green eyes beneath strongly defined, arched brows. Her black hair was pulled back into a classic twist, but strands of it escaped to form a halo of curl around her head.

The gown she wore was basic black, plain in contrast to some of the sequined atrocities that decorated some of the other party goers. But in his memory, the color had been the only thing basic about it. The dress had only two teeny, tiny straps, baring her creamy shoulders, showing off her delicate collarbones and her long, pale neck before molding itself to her breasts and falling over her belly nearly to the floor. It had a sort of stole around it that clipped in the front, right at her breasts, and though she was certainly far better covered than many, he could see that she was generously proportioned in that department. Most generously proportioned. At the time he'd wondered if that was due to her pregnancy, but now he plainly could see that she was still well endowed.

The dancing had begun after dinner. He'd taken Arden onto the floor, and promptly lost her to the attentions of a young man. As he returned to his seat, he'd noticed Patten had taken to the dance floor, too. But instead of holding his lovely wife in his arms, he was wrapped in an indecently close embrace with the executive secretary, whose husband was nowhere to be seen. Deirdre sat alone at their table, a small, forced smile pinned into place, her head high.

A real lady, he remembered thinking. He also remembered thinking that if she were his, the last place he'd be was in the arms of some other woman. Especially when she was pregnant. Any idiot knew women needed reassuring when their bodies were stretched out of shape and their waists were nothing but a memory. No, he'd have to take that back. Her idiot husband obviously didn't know it.

Ronan had taken the seat next to her, but he'd never been good at small talk. Why was it that he could think up dozens of glib lines for his characters to utter, and when he needed them, words always seemed to have dried up? Deirdre had sat beside him in silence, trying gamely to ignore her husband practically having sex with the woman on the dance floor.

Around eleven o'clock the pain had disappeared altogether for a time. Arden had come floating by, whispering in his ear that this might just be The One, and would he mind very much if the fellow took her home, at which he'd laughed and told her to call him in a few days.

He could have left then, but no power on earth would have dislodged him from that table while Deirdre Patten sat there all alone. Finally, when midnight came and her husband was still nowhere in sight, he'd said, "I'd be happy to see you home, Mrs. Patten."

She'd looked at him then, and he had the feeling she was really seeing him for the first time.

"Thank you, but I can call a cab. I'm used to it," she'd said. She'd risen then, and so had he. "Good evening."

There was no reason for him to stay longer, so he'd followed her out of the ballroom. He had no idea when her baby was due but she looked like she couldn't be far away from delivering. God forbid she should fall. Catching up to her in the hallway, he'd offered her his arm at the top of the steps. She'd hesitated, whispered, ''Thank you,'' and slipped her hand into the crook of his elbow.

Outside the front of the lavish hotel in which the party had been held, the doorman hailed a cab at Ronan's signal and he helped her into the back seat. And as the cab drove her away, he'd thought it was a damn shame for a woman like that to be wasted on a jerk like Patten.

Now he waited, a step below her as she unlocked the door to the rooms above the stable. Dressed in a butter yellow tank top tucked neatly into a pair of belted khaki shorts, she didn't resemble the elegant woman from that Christmas party. But as he eyed the neat hourglass figure, the curve of her buttocks beneath the shorts and the thick ponytail that confined most of her black curls, he decided she was equally attractive like this.

He'd fantasized about her for months after the party, picturing her with him, how he'd handle her like spun glass, how she would respond.... It had been a harmless fantasy; he'd never expected to see her again, though he'd wondered if her baby had been a girl or a boy. And, if he was honest, what she'd look like when she wasn't pregnant.

Now he knew. She looked damn good. No, she looked fantastic. Running into her at that store had given him a jolt because she'd looked incredibly close to the way he'd recreated an unpregnant Deirdre Patten in his agile mind.

Immediately, he began hoping that he would see her again and her children...but not because he wanted to get to know *her*. Although she'd been a pleasant, harmless fantasy, he wasn't looking for romantic entanglements. That was the absolute last thing on his mind, of course. No, he was interested in her sons. His knowledge of kids was limited. Being around her children would be exactly what he needed to give life to his current novel. True, the boys were a little younger than the kids he'd first envisioned in the plot he was working on, but it actually would make the story even more compelling if the children were preschoolers.

Her rental property was a stroke of incredible luck. And it wasn't a lie—he was looking for a place to live. Bolton Hill, right in the center of downtown Baltimore, was an enclave of wealth a few blocks wide. But it was surrounded by crime and squalor, and shrinking every year. And while he loved the area, he had found it getting more and more difficult to write in that setting.

He needed space; space to walk and think without the constant vigilance of warding off muggers, to sleep without gunfire and sirens, to work without well-meaning neighbors constantly interrupting his work hours to prove to their friends that a bestselling author really did live next door.

He craved anonymity. He craved the simple ability to walk out of his home without being recognized, a respite from the women who constantly planted themselves at his elbow, hoping for a relationship or even a night with him.

And after the experiences he'd had recently, being hard to locate was highly desirable.

"I warned you." Deirdre stepped aside to let him enter the first room.

She wasn't kidding when she said it needed work, was his first thought. The main room was a large one, with an old wall-mounted sink and an ancient refrigerator at one end—presumably what passed for the kitchen-living area. The floors were unfinished lumber, the walls unpainted. But two skylights as well as a wide window at the near end gave the room a light and airy feel. Through a door at the far end, he discovered a smaller room—a bedroom?—and a bathroom. A real bathroom, with a claw-footed tub and white porcelain fixtures. This room also boasted a large window at its end, though it had no skylights.

Rustic, definitely. But with a few modifications, he could make it work.

"It really is awful," she said from behind him. "I need to fix it up a little before I rent it. It was built more recently than the rest of the buildings here, about sixty years ago when the owner had racehorses. His head groom lived here."

Sixty years ago. Recent, by the standards of the house and the big barn, both of which had to be well over a century old.

Nodding his head, he walked around the empty space. He already knew he was going to take it but he didn't want to appear too eager. Finally he said, "I think it will do if I work on it, add paint and paper, maybe sand the floor."

"You want it?" She eyed him as if he weren't quite sane.

He laughed. "It's solid, looks well insulated. The rest is cosmetic. Would you mind if I fix it up a little?"

"You can do whatever you like with it," she said. "I would offer to reimburse you for any expenses, but—" she swallowed and looked him straight in the eye "—my finances are a bit too strained."

He nodded. "I can understand that."

"You can?" Her expression warmed, and the beginnings of a tentative smile appeared.

"Umm-hmm."

"Money." She sighed. "Life would be so much easier if we didn't have to worry about it."

"Umm-hmm." This was dangerous ground, considering the staggering sum of his last royalty statement.

"Where do you work, Mr.—Ronan?"

Out of habit he searched for an evasion; admitting to being a bestselling suspense novelist had caused him more grief in the past than he could recall. He'd become even more cautious since a fan had been apprehended and eventually convicted of stalking him a year ago. And being anonymous had the added attraction of keeping fortune hunters and celebrity hounds at bay. No, he never told people who he was anymore. It was safer, and less complicated in the long run. And Sullivan was a common enough name that the association didn't come up.

"I'm, uh, sort of a freelance journalist." Well, it wasn't a lie. He'd started out writing articles to support himself while he worked on his first novel.

She nodded, comprehension flooding her expression. "Not exactly a profession you'll get rich at." Then, to his relief, she changed tack. "Cleaning service is included in the rental."

"Uh, that's not necessary. I can clean it myself." If she saw what he already was planning to do to the interior, she'd know for certain he wasn't a struggling writer. He knew that eventually he'd have to tell her the truth, but he hoped the renovated apartment would compensate for his harmless deception. She wouldn't have any trouble renting it after he left.

"Oh, no, I insist—"

"No, I insist." He injected a, "case closed," note into his voice. "You have a business to run and I wouldn't think of letting you waste time on cleaning this place. It's so small I'll have no trouble."

Her brow was furrowed, her eyes troubled. "All right, if you're sure. But if you ever need a hand, don't hesitate to let me know."

"I promise." He held up a hand like a Boy Scout. "Now, how much is the rent?"

Three days later he moved in. Deirdre had told him she was going to be away for the day, taking her sons to a family reunion up in Pennsylvania. She wouldn't be back until well after dark, probably close to midnight, she said. "So don't be alarmed when you hear my Bronco coming down the lane."

The timing couldn't have been better. She left at seven in the morning. As soon as her vehicle was over the ridge, he used his cell phone to call the team he'd hired. Speed was of the essence, he'd stipulated when he'd called the renovation firm. And he didn't mind paying extra for it. When the guy heard that he planned to pay the full amount in cash, he couldn't get the details fast enough.

The paneling came first. He'd chosen a light blond oak because drywall would have to dry before it could be painted or papered; this had to be done in one day. The panels went right over the rough wooden walls, the studs in the original walls providing plenty of support.

Once the paneling in the first room was done, the sub-floor for the carpet went down. The plumber arrived shortly after one o'clock to install the shower and the Jacuzzi, and the guys with the tile for the kitchen and bathroom were right on his heels. By four in the afternoon, he had a rather nice-looking little place, if he did say so himself. The electrician was still working on the dimmers and the surge protection for his office equipment when his new furniture arrived. They were just finishing when the movers arrived with the things he wanted to bring up from his place downtown, and right behind them came the woman from whom he'd ordered the custom blinds and the decorator with art and some stuff like baskets and wreaths for the kitchen walls. It fit perfectly with the casual country feel of the paneling. Lucky for him, the stable windows didn't face the house, or he'd have had to keep the blinds permanently closed.

The last contractor was gone by ten in the evening and he sank down on the new leather couch with a satisfied sigh, looking around him. Amazing. Money worked miracles. He hadn't grown up with it, and he still wasn't used to how easily the thought of extra money could make things move.

Tomorrow the man from the phone company would install his modem line, his fax and telephone. He would unpack his books, get on-line again, and hook up his computer and printer—

The sound of a vehicle growling down the lane was unmistakable. He glanced at his watch—10:09. Wow. He'd just barely made it. He distinctly remembered her telling him she wouldn't be back until late. Since when was a woman ever early?

The next day was Sunday. Deirdre hustled the boys out of bed and they all went to church. Then she turned the car south toward Baltimore. This was the part she hated. The judge had decreed that every Sunday her ex-husband would have visitation rights with Lee and Tommy.

Every Sunday she drove to her friend Frannie's home, where she handed her precious children over to Nelson under the watchful eye of either Frannie, her husband Jack, or both. Nelson wasn't permitted to come near her anymore since she'd gotten the protection order, and the judge had been quite firm in his admonitions. One more little trick and Nelson wouldn't see his sons at all.

She might have to answer for it at the Pearly Gates someday, but she prayed for that one little trick.

Because of Nelson's past behavior, the boys were exchanged at this specified location in front of witnesses. She never wanted to be caught alone with her ex-husband again. Since she'd taken precautions to secure her privacy when she moved out of the house they had once shared, she didn't think he even knew where they lived now. She picked up her mail at a post office in the next little town, had her telephone number unlisted and her business telephone now showed no address. If he had to contact her, he called Frannie and left a message that Deirdre returned. She hated having to instruct Lee and Tommy not to tell their father their address or phone number, but there was no way around it. When she explained that the judge had suggested it, they'd been sufficiently impressed that she doubted their father could bribe the information out of them with ice cream or anything else.

Today went like it usually did. Nelson was waiting for her in front of Frannie's. When she pulled in, Jack came out of the house to greet her. Bless his heart, he must have been watching. She helped her sons out of the car, hugged each fiercely and said, "Have fun with your daddy today." Then Jack took each little hand, and her babies walked down the driveway to the car where their father was waiting.

She was uneasy the entire time the boys were gone, every Sunday. During their marriage, Nelson had saved his worst temper tantrums—her euphemism for abusive rages—for times when he and she were alone. She prayed their children would never know what he was capable of.

As she watched, Lee spoke earnestly to his father before Jack let go of his hand, and she knew he was telling Nelson that she had said it would be nice if he took the boys swimming today. In truth, Tommy was on medication for an ear infection and shouldn't get his head wet, but if she asked his father not to let him swim, they'd go swimming, sure as the moon came up at night. It gave her a small measure of satisfaction to outsmart him. After a few weeks of writing notes that he took great pleasure in crumpling and tossing on Jack's driveway without reading, she'd resorted to this approach when she had instructions she wanted him to hear.

She stood in the driveway waving to her children until the car turned the corner. Then she turned to smile at Jack as he walked back up the driveway. Or tried to smile, anyway. Not an easy feat when your lip was trembling.

Jack lifted an arm and encircled her shoulders loosely as they walked toward the house. "They'll be back before you know it." His voice was a comforting rumble in her ear.

"I know," she said. "But I'm a mother. It's my job to worry." They had a variation on this conversation nearly every Sunday. Time to change the subject—divorce was an ugly, boring topic, and she tried not to inflict it on her friends. "So how's it going with two?"

Jack and Frannie had had a second child five weeks ago—a son. Actually, it was their first, since their daughter Alexa was really Jack's orphaned niece, whom they'd adopted when they were married ten months ago.

Jack looked thoughtful. "I think it's going okay, but I don't really have anything to judge by. Lex was such a piece of cake."

Deirdre laughed. "Must be nice. Neither of my children has ever been a 'piece of cake.'" She stepped past the door that Jack held open for her and entered the home.

"Hi, Dee. Look, Alexa, it's Aunt Dee-Dee."

Alexa was thirteen months old and full of herself, blond and chubby. She ran full tilt at Deirdre, holding up her little arms to be picked up. "An-Dee!"

Catching the little girl up in a fierce hug, Deirdre felt her eyes welling with tears again. Frannie sat in a rocker in the family room with baby Brooks at her breast. She looked serene and happy as she watched her husband, and Dee couldn't help but envy her a little bit. "Never forget how lucky you are," she said, swallowing.

"Lucky to get me," Jack said from behind her. When both women snorted and rolled their eyes, he clutched at his heart and staggered toward the doorway. "Mortally wounded." He straightened and headed for the door to the kitchen. "I know it's a struggle, but if you can bear to be without me, I'm going out to mow the grass."

"Okay, honey," Frannie called after him. "If you do a good job, maybe we'll invite you back later." She exchanged an amused smile with Deirdre. "So how are you? I haven't talked to you all week."

Deirdre shrugged. "Fine. I got another big order from that doll museum in upstate New York. That'll keep me afloat for a little while."

"That's great! This is the third time they've used you, isn't it?" Frannie lifted Brooks to her shoulder and rubbed his back. "Boy, are you a load," she said to him.

"Just like your daddy," Deirdre said, nodding in answer to the previous question. It was true. Little Brooks had weighed a whopping ten pounds, two ounces at birth and showed every sign of being as big as his daddy.

Then Deirdre remembered that she really did have some news. "Oh, guess what? I found a tenant for the apartment."

"Wow!" said Frannie. "That was fast. You just decided to rent it last week. I thought you said it needed some work before it could be rented out."

"It does. But the man says he'll do it himself."

"A man! Do tell."

"His name is Ronan Sullivan," Dee told her.

"And…?"

"And nothing."

"How old?"

"Thirty-five-ish."

"What's he look like?" Frannie's gaze was glued to Dee's face.

Dee thought for a moment. "He's not as big as Jack—who is?—but he's bigger than Nelson. He has dark hair and he seems very nice." *And his hands are warm and gentle.*

"I'm sure I'd be able to pick him out of a crowd based on that description," Frannie said drily. "Are you comfortable having a man on the farm?"

"Not completely," Dee admitted. "But I can't ignore men for the rest of my life. In case you haven't noticed, they're everywhere."

"Well, it's a start." Frannie settled the baby at her other breast. "One of these days you're going to meet some attractive man and realize you're still young. You never know, maybe you'll decide to have a fling with this tenant.''

The words caught her by surprise, sent a rush of purely feminine anticipation through her as Ronan's lean face loomed in her mind's eye. And she realized she'd hesitated a bit too long as she looked over at her friend, whose eyes were alive with open speculation.

Two

On Monday morning she was on the front porch shaking out the rugs when Ronan came around the corner from the side of the stable that faced the woods.

"Good morning." He waved as he altered his path and came toward her.

"Good morning." Deirdre stopped, not sure what else to say. Was she expected to chit-chat with him every time they met? She'd become used to a degree of solitude in the past year; having someone popping up every time she walked outside her house was going to take some getting used to.

"I took a walk down along the creek." He was smiling. "It's really beautiful out here. Very inspiring."

"Inspiring?" She lifted an eyebrow. "Maybe I should have rented that apartment out to an artist."

"It was just an expression," he said as his smile faded. His expression was suddenly guarded, his eyes watchful.

What had she said? She replayed the harmless conversation in her head. Weird. "I'm going to the post office in a few minutes," she said. "Is there anything you want to mail?"

"No." He considered. "But I might go by there later today. I'll have to get directions."

"Sure. There's one in Frizzelburg, although I use another one so I won't be able to pick up your mail for you."

He nodded. "I guess I'd better fill out some change-of-address cards and get a post office box."

"No prob—"

"Woof-woof-woof-woof-woof!"

She was interrupted by a deep, loud barking that grew closer as the dog making the noise zeroed in on her location. "Stand still!" she said urgently to Ronan. "He's not fond of strangers."

Around the corner of the house charged a big, hairy dog, barreling at them full speed. "Murphy, no! Wait!" Her voice was as rough as a drill sergeant's and she stepped in front of her tenant, scowling at the black-and-white dog.

To her relief, her dog halted his mad charge. He stopped about five feet from her and braced his legs; the hair on his back stood up and his canines showed as the barking became a steady, low-pitched snarl. "Quit that," she said, walking over to him. "Sit."

He did both immediately, and she stroked a hand down his nose as she reached him. "Good boy. Lie down."

The big dog dropped to his belly and she gave him a command to stay. Then she turned to Ronan again, aware that her pulse was racing. What must his be doing?

"I apologize. He's usually confined to the house or the fenced area, but the boys must have let him out." On cue, her two sons came tearing around the corner. They stopped dead when they saw her, then slowed and walked toward her at a distinctly unenthusiastic pace.

"Sorry, Mom." Lee's big brown eyes were beseeching. "We just sorta forgot the gate was open."

She hated to scare them, but they *had* to learn to think before they acted. "Mr. Sullivan was taking his walk. What do you think Murphy would have done if I hadn't been out here?"

Tommy's eyes welled with tears and one dripped down his cheek. "Please, Mommy, don't let them take him away. We *promise* to shut the gate next time."

She was aware that her tenant hadn't moved a muscle, and she thanked God he had good sense. And though every cell in her body cried out to her to comfort her children, she knew she had to make sure they understood. "There better hadn't *be* a next time. You may not use that gate. Go through the door on the other end of the porch, remember?"

Two little heads nodded.

"Should we take him back?" Lee asked, indicating the dog.

"No, I need to introduce him to Mr. Sullivan, anyway. But—" she held up a warning finger as her two little terrors turned to scurry away from Mom's wrath "—two beds need to be made and I don't want to find clothes on the floor when I come up to check your rooms."

As they dashed off, she bent and put a hand in Murphy's collar. "If you don't mind," she said to the tenant, "I'd like to let him sniff you so he knows your scent."

Ronan nodded. "That might be wise."

His voice was droll, and she relaxed.

Then, his amber eyes curious, he said, "Why do the boys think someone will take him away if he gets out?"

She couldn't decide how much to tell him, but since the dog was dangerous, it was only fair that he know it. She led Murphy over to him, praising the dog as he thoroughly investigated Ronan and mentally giving her tenant points for not shrinking away. "Murphy bit a man once. But it wasn't Murph's fault. The man was hurting someone and he was only trying to protect me. Anyway, my husband—

my ex-husband—called the police and told them Murphy was vicious, that he needed to be put down.'' She could hear her voice shaking; she stopped and bent her head over the dog, stroking him to give herself a moment. ''The dog warden came and took him away right in front of the boys.''

Ronan made a sound of sympathy deep in his throat. ''No wonder they're upset.'' Murphy was sniffing his hands and he placed them gently on the animal, scratching the big dog's ears. Murphy closed his eyes and leaned against Ronan's legs. ''Obviously he wasn't killed. What happened?''

''He was quarantined for ten days to be sure he wasn't rabid. While Murph was in quarantine, I got a lawyer to help me convince the authorities that the dog wasn't vicious. He was evaluated by two different obedience trainers and two veterinarians. All four said he appeared to be of good temperament, that he has protective instincts and he probably was only acting aggressive under 'appropriate circumstances.' But they also said it was likely he'd bite again if he perceived a threat to me.'' She paused and swallowed, then lifted her head and looked up at Ronan. ''Murphy was protecting me from a close encounter with my ex-husband's temper. He's classified now as a 'dangerous dog,' and if he ever bites again, he'll be put down. He's very wary of strangers now, as you might expect, but I don't believe he would harm you.''

It seemed that her statement was superfluous. Ronan had knelt and was vigorously rubbing Murph's ribs. As she watched, her ''dangerous dog,'' rolled over and let Ronan rub his furry white belly. ''I'd say he likes you,'' she said drily.

''I like him, too.'' He tugged playfully on the immense paws flopping in the air.

''If you ever want to take him along on your walks, feel free.''

Ronan rose and so did Murphy, shaking himself vigorously from head to toe, hair flying everywhere. "I'd love to take him with me sometime. And he could use the exercise, I imagine." Critically he eyed the dog. "He looks like a wolf—is he a husky?"

"He's an Alaskan malamute," she said, fondling Murphy's ear. He leaned against her and she staggered back a step before she could catch herself. "Huskies have blue eyes—mals' eyes are dark brown." She glanced at her watch. "Well. I'd better get to work or the morning will be gone."

"Yeah, me, too." But he made no move to leave, simply stood there looking at her, an odd expression on his tanned features. "I like your dog," he said again, then sketched her a mock salute and turned toward the stable.

Chapter One completed. Ronan all but patted himself on the back as he got up from his desk and stretched. He lanced at his watch. Four-thirty. Time to knock off for a while. He could put in a few more hours later tonight if he felt like it. But he was well under his deadline, so there was no pressure.

He'd been here four days and already those two little hellions had given him enough material to cover the first several chapters. He'd learned that superglue, once applied, is stuck forever, that chocolate bars left in little pants' pockets make a major mess in the washing machine and that when you dig up a dead salamander, its skeleton falls apart.

It wasn't as if he needed that much. A carefully worded sentence here, a phrase there, could give his readers the feeling of knowing his characters. It was more a matter of style, he thought. Each character needed to have a well-defined style. The oldest of the two children in his book was a leader, like Lee. Usually the idea man, the schemer, the one who came up with the ornery ideas. His younger sister—he'd decided at the last minute to make the littler one a girl—was a total tomboy, adoring her big brother and willing to do just about anything he wanted.

And then there was that dog…it would be a real shame not to use that dog in a story sometime. Big Murph, he thought affectionately. He wouldn't use a malamute, maybe a shepherd or a rottweiler, a breed most people could identify.

Her face invaded his mind, and his fingers stilled on the keys. Deirdre had about the prettiest eyes he'd ever seen, a true, clear green set inside thick black lashes that were so long they curled up naturally at the ends. Her eyebrows were strong, for a woman, making a definite statement above those eyes, letting the world know she wasn't as soft as that body suggested, and when she regarded a person with that silky dark brow lifted in cool challenge, it was all a person could do not to respond to it. And speaking of responding…man, what a figure she had! He deplored the anorexic look females seemed to go after these days. Deirdre Patten had big breasts, and her hips, while certainly not wide, were beautifully rounded, just tempting a man to pat them. In between was that teeny-tiny waist, a perfect little shelf for his hands to rest.

For a man's hands, he meant. Any man. Not one in particular.

Hey, there, buddy, he cautioned himself. She might have been your fantasy once, but that's all she's going to be. You have work to do. Besides, she clearly wasn't wealthy and he'd promised himself he'd only chase wealthy women from now on. That way, he'd know they weren't after him for his money.

But she doesn't know you're wealthy. And it's going to stay that way, he told himself. *As soon as you've finished this book, you are outta here.* In fact, he probably should start scanning the ads now, talk to a Realtor, see what was out there, hunt for a little house in a secluded location like this one.

But to do that, he needed to get a newspaper so that would have to wait until tomorrow. Right now, he felt like taking a walk.

He headed down the stairs and started across the yard toward the house. He'd taken Deirdre up on her offer to let Murphy accompany him on his walk the next day, and he'd brought him along every day since. Circling around the end of the house, he walked along a stone path toward the back.

Along the side of the house, huge clumps of peony bushes were in full bloom. Along the fence beside the nearest pasture, a rambler rose like those he remembered from his childhood was laden with pale pink blossoms. A hummingbird feeder full of red nectar swung gently from a tree, and as he let himself through the whitewashed gate in the fence surrounding the back yard, he saw that Deirdre's flowers were starting to unfold their cheery blooms in the raised bed to one side of the yard. She couldn't plant anything along the ground in the backyard, she had explained, because Murphy "christened" everything so frequently that he killed it. Her solution had been to make a box from old railroad ties and fill it with soil, raising the plants above the level of Murphy's frequent markings. In another little touch of which he approved, she had suspended pots of trailing annuals from wrought-iron arms on the fence.

He'd been charmed the first time he saw the backyard, and he felt the same way today. Murphy wasn't in the yard, but a terrific barking from inside the house gave away his location. Just as he began to mount the steps leading to the porch, Deirdre appeared at the back door. When she saw him, she opened the screen and Murphy came bounding down the steps to greet him, jumping and leaping in ecstasy. Obviously the dog had figured out that Ronan equaled "walk."

Deirdre was smiling at his antics as she wiped her hands on a checkered dish towel. Her gaze met his over the dog's bouncing head, warmth and amusement lighting the green to emerald.

God, she was beautiful. Her black hair was loose, the first time he'd ever seen it that way, framing her heart-shaped face in a riotous mass of curls, and when she smiled like she meant it, her eyes slanted into appealing half moons above high cheekbones. She had a little dimple in one cheek and her cheeks and lips were pink and soft look-ing. She was wearing denim overall shorts and beneath them...nothing? For a minute, he had visions of those rounded breasts spilling out the sides of the shoulder straps before he realized she was wearing a skimpy tank top with thin straps beneath.

He had the notion that he must look like a landed fish, gasping for breath, but he couldn't do a damned thing about it. Desire streaked through him, and his body began to stir. He was thankful her dog was so big as he maneuvered Murphy in front of him, and he finally tore his gaze away. "I, ah, I thought I'd take him along with me for a walk again," he said. But as if they had a mind separate from his willpower, his eyes zeroed right back in on her.

Her hands had stilled on the towel and her eyebrows rose in a questioning look. The atmosphere between them sud-denly seemed as intimate as a first kiss; for a minute, she looked as dazed as he felt. Then Tommy appeared behind her, and she turned to slip an arm around her son.

She cleared her throat, staring at the dog rather than Ronan. "That's fine."

He watched her lips form the words, then realized he needed to respond.

"I'll have Murphy back in about an hour," he said slowly. "In time for his dinner."

"Did you eat yet?" Tommy asked him.

Ronan shook his head, smiling at the child. "Not yet. It's a little early."

"Maybe you can eat wif us. I'm helpin' cook a cake."

The little boy looked hopefully up at his mother. "Is there enough spaghetti for Mr. Sullivan, Mom?"

She was looking at him again and he could see the refusal gathering in her eyes.

Whatever common sense he possessed flew right out through the open space between his ears. If there was any way he was going to get a chance to spend more time in her company, he'd take it. "Spaghetti sounds great. If it's okay with your mom." He addressed his words to Tommy, but he was still looking at Tommy's mother.

"You're welcome to join us," she said, breaking the eye contact and looking away, out over the fence at the fields beyond. "We'll call it a thank-you for walking my dog."

He didn't care what she called it. As he turned, he could still see her eyes in his mind, luminous with unanswered questions.

She knew he was returning when she heard Murphy's big feet beat a tattoo on the wooden boards of the porch. She went to open the door for the dog, then held it wide until Ronan had mounted the steps and come inside. As he approached, she saw that he carried a bottle of red wine. "This might go nicely with the pasta," he said.

"Thank you." He was holding out the bottle and she took it, a bit startled as she recognized the label. Her tenant had expensive taste in wines.

He stood just inside the door, taking in the room, and she saw what he was seeing. She'd worked hard to make this house a haven for her and the boys, and she was proud of the end result. Oh, there were any number of things yet that the old house needed, but she felt happy here.

Copper pots hung around the old stone fireplace and a variety of half-burned candles, some rolled from beeswax by the boys, stood on the mantel. A wooden trestle table took up much of one end of the room on an oval rag rug near the fireplace; upside-down bundles of drying herbs and flowers hung from the exposed beams of the ceiling. At the other end of the room, more rugs were scattered over the brick floor, while unobtrusive—but thoroughly modern—black appliances gleamed. Oil lamps, a wrought-iron "tree" full of baskets, a rocking chair with an afghan tossed over the back…this was her kitchen.

She already had set the table with glazed ceramic pottery, a treasure she'd resuscitated after finding it in a box in the attic. Now she said, "Dinner is almost ready. Tommy. Call your brother and wash your hands."

"Not a bad idea," said Ronan.

"There's a powder room on the right down the hall," she said, pointing with the wooden spoon she was about to dip into the spaghetti sauce.

He disappeared behind Tommy, and as he left the room, she felt the invisible presence he seemed to carry around him disappear, too. She'd dreamed about Ronan last night, an embarrassingly detailed dream from which she'd woken aroused and unfulfilled, wondering what it would be like to have him kiss her, touch her. It was only that she'd been alone so long, she had told herself, and he was here, underfoot all the time. And she knew from his concern the night of that abominable Christmas party that he was a nice man.

He was good-looking, despite the way she'd downplayed him to Frannie. His chestnut hair had a reddish cast to it in the sunlight, and his jaw—often stubbled as if he'd forgotten to shave—was square, with a deep dimple right at the bottom of his chin. He towered over her, though that wasn't difficult since she was only two inches over five feet, and she'd noticed that although he gave the impression of being lean, his shoulders blocked the light when he passed through her low doorway. His eyes were like a big cat's, mesmerizing his prey, the golden gaze piercing and direct, ferreting out every secret she thought she had hidden.

The telephone rang as she was putting cheese and a salad on the table.

"Hello?"

"Hello, honey."

"Hi, Mom." She tucked the phone into the curve of her neck as she continued to work. "What's up?"

"I have a favor to ask. Or maybe I'll be doing you one, depending on your point of view." Her mother chuckled. "Your father came home with tickets to the circus for tomorrow. We'd like to take the boys, if you don't have plans. In fact—" her voice warmed enthusiastically as the brainstorm hit "—why don't I come get them and let them spend the night? I can be there in thirty minutes, they'd have a little time to play this evening, maybe take a late swim in the pool, and then they can sleep in tomorrow. We don't need to leave to get to the circus until about ten."

Her mother's timing couldn't have been worse. If she came for the boys in thirty minutes, Deirdre would have to finish the meal alone with Ronan, a situation more awkward than she could imagine. But search as she might, she couldn't come up with a plausible reason to nix the plan. "I guess that would be okay, Mom. If it's all right with the boys."

Both children and their guest had straggled back into the kitchen as she spoke on the phone. She held the receiver to her shoulder and said to Lee and Tommy, "Would you guys like to spend the night with Gramma and Grampa and go to the circus tomorrow?"

Wild war whoops were the answer, and she motioned for quiet as she said to her mother, "I think that's a yes. See you shortly."

Quickly, she got the rest of the meal on the table, adding two wineglasses and handing Ronan a corkscrew as she cut the boys' spaghetti into manageable sizes. She tried not to notice how efficiently Ronan opened the bottle with a few deft twists of his wrist, then slowly and smoothly extracted the cork before filling her glass and his.

"We can dispense with the tasting ceremony," he said.

She made a determined effort to smile casually, nodding in agreement. It felt incredibly strange to be sitting at a table with a man again, although if she was truthful, Nelson had rarely taken family meals with them. Most of the time she and the kids had been on their own.

"So tell us where you've been going when you walk," she said. "Have you found a favorite spot yet?"

He considered the question, but Lee couldn't stand to be quiet for long. "We all have a special spot," he said. "Mine's the big rock up on the hill. It's my fort."

"An' mine's the pine tree clearing," said his brother. "We play we live in there sometimes."

Ronan smiled. For the first time he noticed Lee was missing both top front teeth. His little brother had a lisp a deaf person could hear. They were both so damned cute he thought they could be the kids he saw in commercials. "You'll have to show me your fort and your house in the clearing someday," he said. "Maybe next week you can come with me when I take my walk."

"O-kay!" Lee clenched his fist in the air and drew it down to his side.

"Nelson Lee." His mother was giving him the eye. "You have manners. Use them."

"So." Ronan thought he'd draw fire away from the kid. "Does Mom have a special spot?"

"Uh, not re—"

"Yep." Lee bounced in his chair. "She likes the creek. She takes off her shoes and goes wading sometimes."

"One time we all taked off everyfing and got inna water."

Deirdre made a choking sound. A deep red blush washed up from her neck to her hairline as she said to Tommy, "Do you remember our rule about telling Private Family

Stuff?'' To Ronan she said, ''Don't ever have children. The
whole world hears all.'' She picked up her wineglass and
took a healthy swallow, but he noticed she wouldn't look
him in the eye.

That was okay for now. He sensed her skittishness, and
he wondered if she'd had any relationships since her husband. The idea made him frown. He hoped she hadn't given
any other guy the kind of green light she was giving him
tonight, arranging for her mother to take her kids so they
could have the evening alone. Thinking of what would happen later tonight was a bad move, he decided, shifting in
his chair to ease the sudden tight fit of his shorts. A very
bad move. Purposefully he turned his attention back to the
meal.

Supper was lively, as he'd expected with the little boys
around. He learned that they had both been hospitalized
last summer after they used big, healthy-looking poison ivy
leaves for a ''salad'' they decided to sample outdoors. Lee
proudly showed him the missing space in his front teeth,
courtesy of a close encounter with a swing that he didn't
see coming his way. Tommy showed him a small scar on
the side of his knee where he'd had stitches after he'd fallen
from a tree. He learned that Lee's favorite color was green
and that Tommy slept with a stuffed alligator he'd had
since he was an infant.

''From my father,'' Deirdre explained. ''My father is a
biologist. He's a little…different. How many people do you
know who would pick out a three-foot, stuffed alligator for
a six-pound baby?''

Ronan agreed that it was an unusual gift while he
watched the shift and play of shadow over her smooth ivory
shoulders, bared by the light summer clothing. He was truly
amazed by her children. How she stayed sane keeping up
with these two was beyond him. He'd felt himself sweating
as the boys described their various creative escapades.

But he couldn't keep his mind on the conversation. It

was taking a concentrated effort not to stare at his hostess with his tongue hanging out. She looked like a porcelain doll, he decided. She must garden, because he knew she didn't hire anybody to help out with the yard work, but her ivory flesh looked as though it had never known the kiss of the sun.

When she emptied her wineglass, he refilled it and handed it across to her, and her fingers brushing over his raised goose bumps up his arms in a pleasantly arousing tingle. Even more arousing was the knowledge that the tingle was going to get a whole lot stronger later this evening.

Tommy proudly presented his baking effort for dessert, an angel food cake with lurid green icing made from whipped topping, food coloring and vanilla pudding. He'd seen the frosting recipe in his Sesame Street magazine, he informed Ronan, and Bert an' Ernie made it. Ronan had no idea who Burton Urney was, but he thought the guy should be drawn and quartered for teaching little kids to make disgusting-looking things like that. He tasted it gingerly and was surprised to find it was pretty darn good.

Murphy began to bark as Ronan was finishing his second piece of cake, and Deirdre's mother breezed in the back door. She stopped dead when she saw Ronan sitting at her daughter's kitchen table with Tommy on one knee and a smear of green icing on his cheek.

"Good evening," she said, eyes as striking as her daughter's sweeping over him from head to toe. Though she was quite polite, he could sense the curiosity radiating from her.

Ronan set Tommy on a chair and rose, politely offering his hand. "Hello. I'm Deirdre's tenant, Ronan Sullivan." Deirdre's mother was no taller than her daughter, with an amazingly trim figure for someone he figured had two-plus decades on her. Her hair was snow-white, carelessly anchored in a bun at the back of her head from which stray tendrils escaped and wisped around her head. He was looking at Deirdre in thirty years, he realized.

It wasn't an unpleasant thought.

"Ronan, this is my mother, Maura Halleran," said Deirdre.

"My pleasure, Mrs. Halleran," he said.

When she smiled at him, his heart was lost. "Sullivan," she said, "A good Irish name. When did your family come over?"

"Come over?" As far as he knew, his parents were still safely ensconced in their condo.

"From Eire." Her green eyes were deadly serious. "My grandmother O'Leary was born there. We O'Learys haven't been away that long. The Hallerans abandoned—"

"Mo-ther." Deirdre had obviously heard this before. "Take my children and go before you scare Ronan away. He's a good tenant and if he leaves, who knows what kind of maniac I'll wind up with." She kissed her mother's cheek and herded her and the boys toward the door. "Could be someone like you."

He was still laughing to himself when the boys hollered goodbye and disappeared around the corner of the house with their grandmother, after retrieving the amazing alligator from Tommy's room.

"Wait a minute," he said, belatedly remembering something. "They didn't pack anything. Don't kids still need suitcases?"

"Not for a night at Gramma's," Deirdre said. "She keeps extra sets of clothes there all the time. The only thing that can't be replaced is the alligator."

"Ah." Another tidbit to file away. He never knew when a reference to a grandmother might come in handy in a story.

Deirdre was hovering nervously in the middle of the room and he patted the seat beside him. He'd been anticipating this moment ever since she'd announced before dinner that the boys would be going to their grandmother's

house. "Come sit down. I imagine you don't get many
chances to put your feet up when those two are around."

"You imagine correctly." But she didn't sit down. Instead, she began gathering plates and flatware and fitting
them into the dishwasher. "I'm sorry about my mother.
She's always been interested in Irish history. Well," she
added, "that's the polite way to phrase it."

"I liked your mother," he said mildly as he rose and
gathered glasses, carrying them to the sink. If she needed
some time to ease into his arms, that was all right.

"You don't have to do that," she said.

"Sure I do. You cooked. It's only fair that I help clean
up. Besides, the sooner the table is cleared, the sooner
you'll sit down and relax."

He didn't imagine the startled glance that came his way
as she quickly put away the remains of the meal. But she
didn't comment, just bent and hauled an enormous dog
bowl out from beneath the sink. "I have to feed the big
guy first."

He was riveted to the spot by the sight of her rounded
bottom straining against the seat of her overalls when she
bent over. He could hear his blood roaring through his
veins, could feel his body reacting and he resisted the
strong impulse to grab her by those lush hips and pull her
back against him, to tear off first her clothes and then his,
to plunge into her and let his flesh pound against those
smooth buttocks that would be as porcelain white and soft
as the rest of her until they both were satisfied.

He was hard as a rock now, distinctly uncomfortable in
the shorts that had seemed plenty roomy when he'd put
them on. Turning his back to her, he spotted the wine still
on the table, and on the pretext of retrieving it, used the
opportunity to tug himself into a more comfortable position.
Even the touch of his own hand made his flesh leap and
he closed his eyes, forcing himself to think of his story,
the apartment, his agent's phone call earlier in the

day…anything to keep him from giving in to the primal demand to turn back to that enticing little body this very minute.

His hand shook as he reached for the bottle and the two glasses. "I'll take the wine out on the porch."

"I'll join you in a moment."

He hoped it was a long moment. He hadn't had a reaction like that to a woman since he was about seventeen; he wasn't sure he liked it. But he guessed it made sense. Deirdre had been in his mind for a long time. He'd never expected that he'd ever even see her again, much less be invited into her bed. Well, strictly speaking, she hadn't invited him yet, but why else would she have sent her children away overnight? She wasn't the kind of woman who would carry on with her kids sleeping in the next room, even assuming he would have, which was assuming an awful lot.

The object of his lustful thoughts backed through the screen door then, carrying the dog bowl. Murphy was attached so closely to her side Ronan was sure she would fall over him. But she set down the bowl without incident, and he watched, fascinated, as Murphy gobbled down his dinner in less than ten seconds.

Deirdre shook her head fondly. "Murph, you're a big hog, do you know that?"

The big hog wagged his tail and made a peculiar noise, not a howl, not a growl, more a ridiculous "ru-ru-u," a definite answer to his mistress.

Ronan laughed, and she smiled. "He thinks if he's charming enough, someday I'll give in and let him have more."

She turned and came toward Ronan, and he picked up her wineglass and handed it to her as she sat down beside him on the sturdy, old-fashioned glider. Murphy, seeing his hopes of additional chow dashed, wandered out into the yard to make sure no other dog had invaded his territory.

Deirdre tucked one foot beneath her; the other, he was amused to see, didn't reach the floor. He gently pushed against the floor, setting the glider into a gentle motion.

She didn't speak, neither did he. It was after eight, and the warm June day was finally drawing to a close, the sky dimming and night sounds beginning to filter through the air. A bird called plaintively a time or two, and the rasping of a cricket's wings rose. From a distance the demanding bellow of a frog rhythmically boomed beneath the softer noises.

"It's so beautiful out here." Deirdre's voice was hushed and reverent. "Sometimes I feel like the luckiest person in the world, sitting out here after the boys are in bed, enjoying the peace."

Coming from someone who'd been through what obviously had been a hellish marriage, he thought that was a telling statement. "You feel safe here."

Beside him, she was silent, and he could almost feel the air around her withdrawing. "Some people take safety for granted," she said. "To me, it's a gift."

"How did you find this place?" He wanted her to relax. The aura of tension eased palpably. "My friend's husband knew the previous owner. When he found out I was looking for a place, he thought of this." She paused. "I owe him an enormous favor."

"What kind of favor?" He didn't like the sound of this, friend's husband or not.

She shrugged. "Who knows? It doesn't really matter. I'd do anything—absolutely anything—that he asked." She lifted her glass and drank, and he reached for the bottle and filled it again.

"Lucky guy," he commented.

"Yes, he is." She appeared oblivious to the innuendo in his words. "He's married to one of my best friends, they're so wildly in love it's embarrassing to watch sometimes, and they just had their second child."

He felt a little better. Lifting his arm, he slowly laid it across the back of the glider, casually resting against her shoulder but not completely surrounding her. Yet. "Do you ever think about getting married again?"

"Are you crazy?" She reacted so strongly that he damn near spilled his wine as the swing swayed crazily for a moment. Then she shoved off the glider and he lifted his eyebrows in inquiry. She went to the door and yanked it open for Murphy, who had come up to lie on the rug in front of the screen. His big tail had barely disappeared when she let the door bang shut behind him and spun on her heel. As she stalked across the porch, he could see that she was seething with fury. "I will *never* get married again. You saw what a prince I chose the first time around."

Three

It was the first time she had acknowledged the Christmas party where they'd met. He eyed her back, rigid and frozen where she had come to a halt by the rail, and he realized she was shaking. He hadn't seen her lose it like this. Even when she'd had good reason, at that damned party, she'd been calm and collected, a miserable lady too well-bred to make a scene.

Slowly, he walked across the porch, setting his wineglass on the wide railing. He reached around her and took hers from her and set it down. Then, driven by some instinct that he didn't fully understand himself, he laid his palms on her shoulders, burrowing beneath the cloud of hair and gently rubbing the tense muscles of her neck.

His thumbs stroked and molded, caressed and massaged as he offered her what comfort he could. For long moments he silently kneaded her flesh, feeling the tension ease out of her little by little.

The stiffness in her shoulders relaxed and her body

moved slightly with the pressure of his hands. Her head drooped forward, lolling from side to side, and her hair spilled over his hands. He was getting hard again simply from touching her satiny skin, and he took a deep breath. His hands slowed their massage until he was doing little more than sliding his fingers over the rounded joints of her shoulders.

"I'm sorry," he finally said, bending to offer the words into her ear, stirring curling tendrils of hair with his breath. "We can talk about something harmless, like the weather. Or—" he took her elbow and turned her gently around "—we can forget about talking."

Her eyes were wide and dark in the evening light. The only sign that she'd even registered his words was a slight parting of her lips. Without touching her anywhere else, he lifted his hand and slipped it along her cheekbone, cradling her small face in his palm. She said nothing, only watched him through opaque eyes as he lowered his head and brushed his mouth over hers in the lightest of caresses.

When he touched her lips, he had to restrain himself from devouring her on the spot, so tantalizing and arousing was the contact. An odd feeling spread through him. He'd thought of her so often in this context, but the reality was so much…more. His nerves were jumping and he told himself to calm down and quit overreacting. This didn't mean that much, he assured himself. Even though it felt right somehow, in a way he'd never experienced before.

The second kiss was bolder, firmer, though he deliberately reminded himself to go slowly, take it easy. She made no move to resist him, but he felt her mouth begin to stir, moving beneath his until he insistently thrust his tongue into her depths. She gasped. He pulled her against him, his arms wrapping around soft curves, his body meeting hers from shoulder to hip. For the first time, she touched him, putting her small hands tentatively to his shoulders, then sliding them around his neck as she allowed him to kiss her, and kiss her, deepening the contact with each stroke of his tongue.

He took his mouth from hers, sliding his lips over the fine line of her jaw to her ear, where he pressed a string of small kisses that descended the smooth column of her long neck, across her collarbone and farther, to the hollow at the base of her throat and the tender skin below it. He felt her swallow, and he moved down, over her breastbone and beyond. The rough fabric of the front bib of her overalls stopped him and he took it in his teeth, tugging gently for a moment until his mouth moved on, repeating its journey in reverse and he moved up the opposite side of her neck and back to her mouth again.

He felt like a king. She was flesh and blood, a living woman filling his arms, everything he'd dreamed of and a million things he hadn't even imagined.

Her scent. She smelled fresh and clean, a faint, elusive flower smell that made him think of spring rain and budding things. It was stronger when he tore his mouth from hers and buried his face in her hair, savoring the sweet pressure of her female form against him.

Her hair. The wild curls were surprisingly soft and silky, caressing his face and clinging to the stubble of his chin when he drew back, billowing around her shoulders and brushing a fine curtain of living satin over him.

Her flesh. He'd imagined her soft, like a comfortable pillow. But he hadn't envisioned the undeniable play of muscle in her arms, the slenderness of her torso, the way her hipbones jutted forward to tantalize him.

He was hard, aching for her. Without volition, his hips moved against her, grinding his throbbing flesh against her belly, an unsatisfactory caress that only inflamed his need.

He kissed the side of her face, her ear, her shoulder again, and her head fell back, like a wilting flower on the long stalk of her neck. "I can't think," she whispered, and her voice was a slurred murmur in the dusky evening.

"You don't have to think," he whispered against the exposed underside of her chin, trailing openmouthed kisses down to the frustrating impediment of her clothing again. "Just feel." He took one arm from around her, splaying wide the fingers of his other hand to hold her closely against him, though she was doing a pretty fine job of plastering her body to his without any help. His free hand came to the shoulder strap of her overalls, fumbling with the closing for a few seconds, then impatiently pulling it down to give him better access to her sweetness. She lowered her arm long enough to pull her elbow free, then put it back around his neck and he repeated the motion with the other strap.

All that stood between him and those glorious mounds of femininity now was a thin white camisole that buttoned down the front; its straps had come down when he pulled the overall straps away. He got both his hands between them, fumbling open the damnably tiny buttons, while he continued to kiss her neck. She didn't help him in any way, but she didn't halt him, either, keeping her arms loosely linked around his neck and allowing him to touch her as he willed.

Her passive acceptance only inflamed him; he shoved the last button on the camisole through its stubborn hole, then spread wide the garment to expose her breasts and drew back to examine the results of his labor. The bib was bunched at her waist; all she wore was a strapless bra—fancy underwear for a farm girl—that clasped in the front. His eager fingers met between her breasts and she whimpered as the bra fell away.

For the first time, he sensed her withdrawing from him, but as she began to slide her arms from around his neck, he raised his hands and clasped her wrists, holding them in place. He sought out her lips again, kissing her deeply until her tongue danced with his again and her hips beat a gentle tattoo against his insistent arousal. Slowly, he eased his mouth from hers and leaned back, examining the results of his work of a few moments ago.

If he were a dying man, he'd give up the ghost without a peep of protest. Her breasts were beautifully large and rounded, pale nipples spreading to crown each upthrust point. Though their color was indistinguishable in the darkening approach of night, in his mind's eye they were smooth, white cream, the crests a pale rose with slightly darker tips. He put both hands to her, covering them with his palms, hefting the sweet weight and running his thumbs back and forth across the tips until her nipples rose in response to his command. His lips beat a voracious path down across the yielding flesh to suck a nipple into his mouth. He laved it with his tongue, continuing to stimulate the other with his thumb until she began to writhe against him and he thrust his leg forward, parting hers and shoving her up until she was riding his leg, the long muscles in his thigh beneath her sensitive woman's mound giving her what she craved.

His own body was growing too insistent to ignore, and he unbuckled his belt and unzipped his pants while still suckling her. Then he stepped back a small pace, depriving her of her saddle. She whimpered again and the small sound sent him over the edge. Frantically, he grasped the overalls, dragging them down her legs, tearing a pair of tiny lace panties down in the same motion. Another time, he might have stopped to appreciate the pretty sight, but now he was blind and deaf to anything except what he needed.

And what he needed was her.

He caught her under the arms as he pivoted so that he sat propped against the edge of the porch rail. In the same moment, he lifted her, pulling her against him. Her arms tightened around his neck, and he held her to him with one arm around her bottom while he reached between them and freed his desperately straining male flesh from its prison. He slid his hand between her thighs and pulled one leg up around his waist, and she followed suit with the other, clasping her legs around his hips, trusting him to support her. He groaned as the motion ground his sensitive shaft against the exposed cleft between her legs and he felt a slick moisture that told him all he wanted to know.

He grasped himself, guiding his engorged flesh to her, probing for the entrance to her deepest secrets. She cried out and wriggled against him, and with a sudden movement he plunged into her up to the hilt.

They both sucked in a startled breath.

He had intended to ease into her, to give her time to accept him, to let her body stretch until she could comfortably accommodate him. The incredible sensation of being suddenly surrounded, engulfed and captured in one smooth joining was so exquisite that he nearly spilled his seed right there, but he wanted her with him, wanted to see her face as he gave her her own ultimate pleasure and he forced himself to a long moment of stillness until he had recovered his control. He began to thrust slowly, gritting his teeth at the mounting pressure, at the way her tight channel clung around him. He pulled her hips to him, letting her breasts jiggle and bounce against his chest as she braced her hands on his shoulders. Her eyes were closed and he wanted to see her, wanted her to see him.

"Open your eyes," he growled, in a voice nearly unrecognizable even to himself.

Slowly, the thick screen of her lashes lifted, and she raised her eyes to his. He gazed into the depths of passion, dark and hot as the night around them. Then he placed his hand between them again, his thumb moving unerringly to cover the pouting bump that had risen within her nest of curls. She jerked, her eyes flaring wide, and he bared his teeth as her unconscious tensing squeezed him in a deep internal caress his flesh was racing to answer. Mercilessly, he circled her body's most sensitive site, eyes locked on hers in an incredibly intimate communion, until she began to shudder, her legs convulsively clutching around his hips. He had been moving steadily within her, but the sounds, the sight and the sensation of her climax triggered his body's own rush to fulfillment, and he moved strongly against her, holding her hips in his hands, his own body pounding a frantic gallop to pleasure, until he found his own peak, feeling the sweet relief that accompanied the jetting of his seed, the wracking spasms that drew his body into a rigid arch of tense energy before he blew out a deep breath and sagged against her, burying his face in her neck.

After a moment he felt strength returning. Without moving her from his body, he walked to the glider and sat down, loving the motions of his flesh within her, realizing, to his astonishment, that he could do this again with very little provocation.

She had said nothing the whole time, simply laid her head on his shoulder when he sat, her arms lying heavily around his neck. He turned his head and kissed her forehead just because he could, savoring the moment. He felt as if he'd been waiting for this all his life. But how did she feel?

"What are you thinking?" he asked, trying to keep a casual note in his voice.

She was quiet for a moment, then she said, "That this was the most incredible experience of my life. That I drank way too much of that wine." He felt her sigh. "That this is the most awful situation I've ever been in in my whole life."

He was startled, and the smug pleasure he'd felt at her first sentence evaporated. "Coming from you, that's a serious insult. What was so awful about it?"

"Nothing was wrong with *it* —"

"Good. I agree."

"It's the *now* I'm talking about."

It was almost surreal, resting on the glider, their cooling flesh still melded together as they murmured in the darkness. She made no move to end the intimacy and he gathered her closer, running his palms up and down over the satiny textured skin of her back. He gently thrust his hips against her once, hoping to distract, reassure. "The 'now' doesn't feel so bad to me."

"You know what I mean. This is going to ruin our…business relationship."

"Why? What does this have to do with me renting an apartment from you?"

"It's just awkward. Every time I see you, I'm going to be thinking of this. I won't be able to look you in the eye."

"It doesn't have to be awkward." What the hell was wrong with her? It wasn't like he was planning for this to be a one-night stand.

"I've never done casual sex," she wailed into his chest "What was I thinking?"

"You weren't, remember?" He was getting irritated. This had been about the best damned thing that had happened to him in years, and she was ruining it. "We're two people who knew we'd be terrific together and we acted on it. There was nothing wrong with that."

"It was wrong," she said in a shaky voice. "I can't take chances with my life. I have children to consider. I know nothing about you and I let you, let you…" She stumbled over the words and he finished the sentence for her.

"You let me have sex with you."

"Yes." Her voice was a whisper.

"Would you like me to take an HIV test?" Obviously sex was all it had been for her. For him, it had been…he didn't know, but he knew she had been more than just another body. It was an uncomfortable realization; he pushed it away as a thought struck him. "That's not the only chance we took." Grimly he held her when she would have pulled away. "You're not using any birth control, are you?"

Her eyes narrowed as she absorbed his words and their impact struck; she shook her head.

"Let me know if you're pregnant."

"Oh, God, I hope not." She averted her face; he sensed her withdrawing again.

Though his flesh was still snug within her, she suddenly seemed as far away and unattainable as the moon. Exasperation rose, along with a stupid sense of hurt, and he grasped her by the waist and lifted her to the glider beside him, then rose and righted his clothing. He zipped his shorts with a vicious hiss as he strode to the edge of the porch where her clothing lay strewn over the floor. Grabbing her things in a bundle, he tossed them at her, then crossed his arms and leaned against the railing where, a few moments ago, he'd felt like the happiest guy in the world.

"For somebody that set this up on purpose, you sure have changed your tune."

She paused in the middle of hitching her overalls up. He noticed that she hadn't bothered to put her underwear back on beneath the little top and the denim; she had stuffed them into one pocket, from where they peeked out. "What?"

"You heard me."

"What do you mean, 'set this up on purpose'?" Too late, he recognized shock and rising anger in her husky voice.

He shrugged, though he was feeling distinctly uneasy. This hadn't gone quite as he'd expected. Or as he'd hoped. "You didn't have to spell it out. Why else would you have called a baby-sitter to take your kids off your hands?"

He'd never seen anyone literally speechless before. If he hadn't been emotionally invested in this scene, it would have been fascinating. Right now, it made him wary as hell. Her mouth opened, closed and opened again. Her eyes widened, then narrowed and she shot him a look that made him glad she didn't have a weapon handy.

She clenched her fists at her sides, her entire body rigid as she said, "I did not ask my mother to take my children away so that I could seduce my tenant. She called me. For your information, I almost didn't let them go because they're already away from me every Sunday with their father.'' She turned on her heel and stomped to the back door, practically spitting fury as she yanked open the door. ''You're not that irresistible.''

''Seemed like it a few minutes ago.'' It was a nasty thing to say but he was feeling nasty. For him, this had been the beginning of something he sensed could have been very special. Not permanent—that was his cardinal rule—but still, special. His dream was being ripped away from him before it even began.

He heard her gasp, and the door slammed behind her. The sound of a lock clicking into place was loud in the quiet of the summer evening. He felt like kicking something.

Then he heard a suspicious sound. Was she crying? Remorse overrode his frustration. He'd never forgive himself if he'd made her cry. How had this gone so wrong? ''I'm sorry,'' he said through the door. ''Please come out and talk to me.''

''Go away.''

She was definitely crying. Damn. He hesitated, anger and anxious concern warring within him. She'd be even less enchanted with him if he broke her door down. Fine. He stomped down the steps as Murphy began to bark. It was a wonder she hadn't sicced her damned killer dog on him.

Halfway across the yard, he realized he hadn't told her who he really was yet.

The last time she'd cried had been over a year ago, after she tried to comfort her oldest son when his father had forgotten his birthday for the first time.

The last time she'd cried for herself had been even longer ago than that.

But tonight she was making up for it. She lay in her

pretty brass bed in the pretty room she'd decorated to suit herself, and she sobbed. Out loud. No need to cry into a pillow; there was no one to hear her.

No one. The two loneliest words in the English language. She'd been a nice person growing up, she thought. She hadn't been a mean or vengeful child; she'd never been the kind of girl whose chief pleasure lay in tearing others less fortunate to bits. She'd been a good student, a good daughter, a good mother. Not perfect at any of the above, maybe, but not a total zero, either.

So why had her life been so totally stinking rotten in the past few years? What had she ever done to deserve to have men treat her like dirt?

She rolled over onto her side, curling into a miserable ball.

Never again. Never again was she going to let a man get under her skin, slice at her feelings, trample her soul. Her marriage had been a farce for most of the not-quite-three years she'd lived as Mrs. Nelson Patten. Tonight she'd let a man she barely knew seduce her with his eyes, with his admiration and skillful kisses, until she'd been like a cat in heat, rushing headlong into sexual pleasure.

She barely recognized her own behavior. There was no excuse. But it had been so nice, so very nice, to see admiration in a man's eyes when he looked at her. To see desire and passion and need. And to know that a man could make her want him, too.

She'd been giddy from the wine, but she couldn't blame that. Ronan Sullivan was the most sexually compelling man she'd ever met. Just being in the same room with him made her feel jumpy and jittery and aware of her own feminine sexuality.

He'd been polite and pleasant and perfectly correct for most of the time she'd known him. But after the boys had left with her mother, the atmosphere had changed. She'd recognized the shift, felt his intense interest; his kiss hadn't been unexpected.

Or unwelcome, either, if she were truthful with herself.

No, she hadn't been averse to being kissed. She had actually looked forward to it, to experimenting with a few little caresses as her first step in becoming a single, dating woman. She just hadn't been expecting every brain cell she had to go on vacation when he had touched her. She hadn't been expecting the huge flare of need that erased all thought from her head and urged her to twine herself around him like a piece of cling wrap.

Wearily she rolled onto her back again.

Crying never helped anything. Except maybe to purge her of the worst of the pain. Tomorrow would be here as soon as she fell asleep. Tomorrow she would work in the morning, get her children back in the afternoon and do what she usually did in the evening: housework, laundry or more sewing. An exciting Saturday night.

She was awakened the next morning by Murphy standing beside the bed, panting heavily. It was his "I need to go out" pant, and she pulled herself out of bed and shuffled downstairs to let him out into the yard. She showered, dressed and braided her hair—it really had been too hot yesterday to wear it loose.

She opened the refrigerator door and stood, staring without seeing, until the cold air reminded her and she removed the orange juice. While she was making herself a slice of toast, the telephone rang.

"Hello?" It was early, but everyone knew she got up at the crack of dawn, so it wasn't unusual.

"Hi, Dee!" It was Frannie.

"Good morning." She could hear the baby fussing in the background. "Sleepless night?"

"Yeah, but Jack was the one pacing the floor," her

friend said with distinct glee. "Listen, are you going to be around today?"

"Yes."

"I have a really strange request from a customer and I need your help. Mind if I run out this afternoon?"

"Not at all. I'd love to see you. There's only one condition."

"Oh?"

"Your entry fee is the baby."

Frannie laughed. "Not a problem. Until he's weaned, we're stuck with each other except for brief escapes to the grocery store."

"I remember those days." Thinking of nursing her own babies brought a sweet swell of feeling. She'd loved every moment of those baby days.

Baby.

Ronan. A breathless dread crept through her.

Cusses. She was doing her best not to think about him this morning. With determination she finished the conversation, let Murphy back in and fed the big lug, then started toward the old sunporch she'd converted into her sewing room. The New York order was a significant one; the sooner she completed it, the sooner she'd get paid.

She worked straight through lunchtime, only remembering it when the dog began to get restless. Oh, well, it wasn't as if she was going to waste away to nothing if she missed a meal. Standing at the sink, she peeled an apple and ate it slice by slice. She was just washing her hands when Murphy let her know someone was coming.

Frannie's van was pulling to a halt in the lane when she walked out front. Murphy was bouncing around the vehicle, barking and ru-ruing like he did when he recognized a friend, tail slapping from side to side. The driver's door opened. Frannie stepped out and waved, then walked around to the passenger side to get the baby.

Then the front passenger door opened. A blond head appeared, followed by a slim, shapely figure who walked forward with her arms out. "Hi, honey!"

"Jill! When did you get back?" Deirdre hurried to hug her other closest friend, who had been on a cruise for the past few weeks.

"Last night. Late. I called Frannie this morning, and when I found out she was coming out, I horned in." She released Deirdre and stooped to throw her arms around Murphy's thick neck in a rough-and-tumble hug. "Hello to you, too, you dumb dog. Quit slobbering on me."

"Come on in." She felt happier than she had all day. She turned to ask Frannie if she needed help carrying anything in, but a movement caught the corner of her eye and she automatically turned to look. So did Jill and Frannie.

Ronan had walked around the corner of the barn, headed for the woods. When he saw them, Jill waved enthusiastically. He hesitated a moment, then began to walk toward them.

"Whoa! *Where* did you get *that?*" Jillian's tone was hushed as she brushed dog hair off the aqua sleeveless top that made her gorgeous tan glow. She shoved her huge red-framed sunglasses to the top of her head for a better look.

Frannie whistled under her breath. "Is that your tenant? You lucky, lucky girl."

"Hey, none of that. He's off-limits to married mothers," Jill said. "Anyone have a tissue? I'm drooling."

Deirdre took one quick look, their gazes meeting for a fleeting second before hers bounced away. He was wearing faded gray sport shorts of some soft fabric that clung to his body and a navy sweatshirt whose arms had been cut out by a haphazard hand. As usual, he needed a shave, and his chestnut hair gleamed in the sun. His muscles bunched and flexed like a big jungle cat as he strode toward them, the shorts hiding not one detail of his blatantly male physique.

"Good afternoon, ladies." Ronan stopped a few feet away. His tone was smooth and cordial, but he didn't smile.

"Jill, Frannie, this is Ronan Sullivan. He's renting the apartment over the stable."

"Dee!" Jill's tone was horrified. "That place is a rat trap." She stepped forward and extended her hand to Ronan, smiling coquettishly. "I'm Jillian Kerr. If that old stable is too rustic for you, I could probably find room for you at my place. You give me a call and I'm sure I can find something to do with you."

Ronan's eyebrows rose and he finally smiled. "I just bet you could."

If he'd wanted to twist a knife into her, he couldn't have done a better job. Last night had been special to her, even if Ronan only started it because he thought she was giving him a green light. How could he flirt with her friend right in front of her? Even though she knew Jillian was joking, charming him effortlessly as she did with every man she met, a fist of denial clutched at her throat. She hated the thought of Ronan flirting with anyone. The tears she thought she'd finished with last night rose hot and thick behind her eyes, and she looked at the dusty stones on the ground before her, willing them back into whatever bottomless reservoir they came from.

"I'm Frannie, and this little sumo wrestler is my son Brooks." When Deirdre didn't speak, her other friend introduced herself.

Deirdre finally looked up again as Ronan murmured something conventional in return. Her friends both were casting her curious glances. Ronan's face was stony again and his eyes went hard and flat when he turned to her. "I'm going for a walk now. May I take Murphy along?"

"Yes, thank you. He needs to work off some of his excess energy today."

"Me, too."

His tone wasn't suggestive, but a picture of his hard chest, the washboard muscles of his stomach, rose to taunt her. She knew she was blushing, and she turned away quickly, addressing her friends. "Come on in. This heat can't be good for Brooks."

No one spoke until they entered the house and walked back to her kitchen. She hurried to a cupboard and got out glasses. "Lemonade all right with you two?"

Jillian nodded.

"Ice water for me, please. A big glass. Since I started breastfeeding, my mouth is always as dry as cotton." Frannie cleared her throat. "You and your tenant certainly are polite to each other."

"I thought perhaps I detected a certain…tension…in the air," Jillian suggested. "But surely I was mistaken."

Deirdre kept her eye on the glasses she was filling. "You must have been."

Jill laughed. "Dee, honey, you're not fooling us. I can spot attraction a mile away. What is going on between you and our handsome Ronan?"

She couldn't tell them. Not even these two, her dearest friends in the world, who had seen her through the hellish days of her divorce and supported her when she thought she just couldn't be strong anymore. "It's— I—I'm sorry," she managed, her voice shaking. "It's not something I can talk about right now."

There was a moment of astonished silence.

Then Jillian moved to her side, wrapping an arm around her shoulders. "It's okay, honey. You know where we are if you need us."

Frannie nodded, her eyes sympathetic. Then she turned to the diaper bag she carried everywhere, pulling a sheet of sketch paper from a pocket. "Here. Before I forget why I came out here in the first place, take a look at this. I have a customer who wants to have an exact replica of her wedding gown made for a Barbie doll."

Deirdre took the paper, concentrating on Frannie's words while she gathered her composure. "I don't normally design for the eleven-inch dolls, but I probably could do this. It might be fun. What fabrics are you using?''

Jillian reached for the baby. ''You two go right ahead and talk sewing. It's mumbo-jumbo to us, isn't it, Brooks-buddy? Let's go play with some toys.''

Three weeks later her New York order was almost finished. The clothing for eighteen-inch specialty dolls had been ordered by a nationally known toy store for its display window. The scene was a winter one around a frozen pond, so the dolls had to be garbed in layers and layers of clothing. She'd even made tiny leather ice skates, and knitted eensy-weensy mittens, mufflers and hats.

She was anxious to get the order finished. Not only because of the money, which would be welcome, considering that she had a balloon payment on her mortgage due next month, but also because she planned to work Frannie's customer's Barbie doll wedding dress in before she started another order. The fabrics would be a challenge in miniature, and she needed a challenge to occupy her mind right now.

She was consumed by worry these days, unable to focus her attention on anything for long before her troubled thoughts intruded again. What if she was pregnant? She'd soon be able to take an early pregnancy test. And then she'd know. If only she were able to wave a wand and make time fly forward a few weeks.

If course, if she could make time fly, she also could go backward. And be smart, sensible and sober. Then she wouldn't be ''what-iffing'' herself to death.

What would she do if she were going to have a baby? Another child would strain her resources almost beyond her ability to provide for her family, even if her lawyer ever succeeded in getting Nelson to pay her for the months of child support he'd ignored so far. She really needed another two or three years to get her business solidly entrenched, and if she had an infant, it would be even harder to devote the time she needed to her projects.

But there was no question in her mind about what she would do. She could never terminate a life. No, if she was pregnant, then her family would have a new member. She knew she would love another child when it arrived, but right now she was praying one wouldn't arrive at all.

The evening with Ronan had receded in chronological time, but in her memory, every detail was as fresh and clear as if he'd just taken his hands from her body. It still bothered her to admit she'd been so easy. That was a word reserved for other women, women who frequented bars seeking out the very thing she wished she could erase from her life.

But in a strange way, though she regretted her behavior, she had made peace with the memories. She didn't regret that she no longer thought of Nelson, of silently staring at the ceiling and enduring when he decided to remind her that she was his wife. And she didn't regret that she knew now how shiveringly, excitingly intense the act of coupling could be with a man who was tuned in to her responses. Her body tingled just thinking about it. About him.

She'd barely seen Ronan since. He came to take Murphy for his walk and they exchanged a sentence or two through the screen door. Occasionally she saw the boys chasing after him and she would call them in. She didn't want her children bothering him.

He closeted himself away in the stable most days. It made her wonder if he wasn't having much luck with whatever kinds of things he was writing. Still, he had had no problems so far paying his rent, so she supposed it wasn't her problem. Or her business.

"Hey, Mom!" Lee charged into her sewing room, narrowly avoiding a stack of new fabrics she'd just received.

"Careful, hotshot," she cautioned. "What do you need?" The boys had been watching a movie in the next room, and she'd been pleased that they were being so quiet. Sometimes she had to resort to working after they were in bed, because they were under her feet too much during the day. She felt a dull guilt each time she had to refuse them an ounce of her time because she had to work, but right now there was no help for it.

"You gotta help us cut up the watermelon." Wide brown eyes beseeched her to come right now and help.

"What watermelon?" They pretended all the time; she just went along with the make-believe scenarios if they weren't dangerous.

Lee regarded her impatiently. "Ronan's watermelon."

"All right." Her sons were enthralled with Ronan; the more she enforced the Let's Not Bug the Tenant rule, the more desperately they wanted to be with him. She supposed that if they had to talk about him, she'd go along.

Lee took her hand when she rose from her chair, practically dragging her through the house and out the back door. When she saw Ronan standing on the porch, an enormous watermelon cradled in his arms, her heart leaped into her throat.

"Hello." She was proud that her voice sounded so calm. He was wearing another shirt with the arms cut off but this one also had been hacked off at the waistband; at least, she assumed that was where it originally had been intended to fall. It obviously had been washed a few hundred times since then, and now it barely reached to the middle of his broad chest. The muscles in his arms bulged. Below the shirt, a tanned torso was bisected by a thick arrow of dark curly hair running vertically into the waistband of his shorts.

She wanted to reach out and touch so badly that she curled her fingers into fists and dug her nails into the palms of her hands.

"Hi." His voice was deep, his golden eyes intent. "I won this at the little market up the road."

"You...won it?"

"Yeah. The lady who owns the market got a truckload in and this one was so much bigger than all the rest she decided to raffle it off and give the proceeds to the Cancer Society. I only bought a ticket to be polite."

"Looks like you should be polite more often." It had been a flippant response; purely off the top of her head.

So when his eyes met hers and he quietly said, "I think so," she didn't have a response. There was a double meaning hidden in there somewhere, she was sure, but the look in his eyes confused her, and she was afraid to think about what that look might mean.

"You can borrow one of my bigger knives to cut it up," she offered.

He shook his head. "Too lazy. I gave it to Tommy and Lee."

"Oh." She turned to her sons. "Did you say thank you?"

"They did," Ronan confirmed.

"Mommy, are we gonna watch firewoks on the Fouwf of July?" Tommy cocked his head in inquiry. "Aunt Jill told me firewoks comes soon."

Deirdre nodded, a little confused by the sudden change of topic. She wanted to end this conversation. "Three more days," she confirmed. "I guess we'll go up on the hill like we did last year. Did you like that?"

Tommy nodded. "And take a picnic like last year."

"Mr. Sullivan, you can come with us," said Lee. "On the picnic. You'll really, really like the fireworks."

"Oh, boys, I'm sure Mr. Sullivan has plans for the Fourth." This was her own fault. If only she hadn't taught her children to be so cussed friendly. She looked at Ronan over her sons' heads, waiting for him to acknowledge the easy out she'd given him.

"Actually," he said, "I don't."

Four

What did he think he was doing? she asked herself silently on the Fourth as she sliced his watermelon into manageable chunks for her children. Having a picnic with Ronan, even with the distraction of her sons, would be a true test of endurance. She couldn't think of anyone she'd rather picnic with less.

Liar.

It's the truth, she told herself, slicing vigorously.

Come on, Deirdre, admit it. There's nothing wrong with admitting to a little bit of lust. Except that you wish it wasn't just lust.

She sighed as she packed the watermelon into a container and placed it in the cooler. It must be a girl thing, to romanticize every guy who comes close. She had proof positive that Ronan was no Prince Charming, and yet she had caught herself daydreaming at least once a day, reveries in which he became the perfect second husband, adoring her, adoring her children from her first marriage—

That part really was a fantasy, she told herself. Yesterday, she'd been weeding around the front of the house when a loud, close crash nearly stopped her heart. Looking around, she'd seen that the bottom pane of the window just to her right was shattered. She'd known, even before she'd called for the boys, that they must have gotten a little carried away with their game of catch. Still, she hadn't thought either one of them was big enough to be breaking her windows yet.

When she called them, to her surprise they emerged from the house. She'd checked not fifteen minutes ago, and they'd been playing in the grassy field behind the back fence. "What happened?" She could see from their faces they weren't hurt.

"What happened?" Ronan came jogging over from the stable. He eyed the broken living room window. "How'd you do that, guys?"

Lee took a deep breath. "Well, we went in the house for a drink of water—"

"And we saw dat fan."

Fan? Her eyes widened. "What fan?"

"The one in the living room," Lee said.

"Onna ceiling," clarified his accomplice.

"We just wondered if it could hit a baseball, so we threw the ball up a couple of times while the fan was on." Lee spread his hands as if his logic would have occurred to any one.

"An' it did!" Tommy's face glowed for a second before he remembered the results of the experiment.

She'd sent them to their rooms, unimpressed with their scientific bent.

When she'd turned around, Ronan had been shaking with laughter. "I'm getting quite an education from watching those two."

She hadn't seen anything funny about it. The window had been extremely old, the kind of beautiful wavy glass that actually had bubbles in it. "I'm going to have gray hair by the time I'm forty."

Ronan had still been chuckling, shaking his head as he'd walked away. Sure, he might think they were cute. But if he lived with them full-time, she thought as she finished packing the cooler, she doubted he would adore them.

In fact, that was one of the reasons she never thought she'd marry again. Not only because the mere thought repelled her, but because of Tommy and Lee. They were a handful, but she still loved them. Someone who wasn't their biological father would have a harder time with things like broken windows, spray-painted bedroom walls and miniature trees and houses glued to the floor to make a village.

She closed the cooler and took a deep breath. Time to go. Lifting it, she carried it to the back porch, then went back for the picnic basket. As she locked the door, the boys came squealing back along the stone path.

"Hey, Mom, are ya ready yet?" Lee had asked her that approximately fifty times in the past three hours or so.

"Yes, I'm ready." She dropped her keys in her pocket and put both hands on the handle of the cooler.

"All right!" Lee disappeared as fast as he'd popped up, with Tommy hot on his heels.

"I'll get that." Ronan had followed the boys back up the walk.

She shook her head. "That's all right. I have it."

But he stepped right in front of her as if she hadn't spoken, forcing her to stop as he removed the cooler from her. She had to surrender it or allow his hands to cover hers on the grips, and she wasn't about to get that close to him. He settled the cooler on one hip, then hefted the picnic basket in the other hand. "Do you want these in the back of the Bronco?"

"Yes, please." Scurrying around him, she led the way to her vehicle. When she opened the back, he set the cooler in, turned and did the same with the picnic basket. Then he reached for a bag sitting beside the rear tire with two lawn chairs. As he set it in the Bronco, she asked, ''What's that?''

He hooked a finger in the edge of the bag and tilted it toward her. ''Sparklers. And a few other small kinds of fireworks. I didn't want to show the boys until I'd cleared it with you.''

Her first instinct was to say no. Fireworks terrified her, no matter what size. She'd had a playmate who had lost two fingers when a small firecracker had exploded in his hand. For that matter, fire terrified her. She'd never been one of those children who had played with matches. The mere sight of a small leaping flame made her apprehensive. Even burning the candles in her kitchen made her too tense to leave the room while the tiny wicks were lit.

But she knew the boys would be thrilled. And she also knew that Ronan wouldn't let them near anything that might harm them. Slowly she said, ''I suppose it would be all right. As long as they don't actually handle anything except the sparklers.''

He nodded. ''I wouldn't let them near any of the other stuff. I just thought they might enjoy having their own personal fireworks display.''

She was touched. ''Thank you,'' she said.

When he shrugged and said, ''Sure,'' she reached out, without thinking, and put a hand on his arm. His flesh was covered with fine silky hairs, warm and firm beneath her palm and immediately, an involuntary charge of arousal detonated deep in her womb. She jerked her hand away, but she knew from the intent look on his face that he'd discerned her reaction. His eyes dropped to her mouth. It wasn't fair, she thought, that he could get her so excited that she forgot everything but him.

Looking away, she stepped back a pace and fought to recall the conversation. ''I really appreciate your thoughtfulness,'' she said. And she did. Nelson never would have thought of doing anything simply for the sake of his sons. In fact, she really didn't think he would take any time for them except for the fact that he knew it bothered her. He'd become incredibly vindictive since she'd left him.

It wasn't until she was in the driver's seat of the Bronco, bouncing through the lower field, that it occurred to her that she trusted Ronan with her children, trusted him enough to permit him to introduce her children to fireworks. Trusted him more than she did her children's own father.

They settled under a big oak tree standing isolated and majestic on the highest hill on the property. The grass was green and the ground was soft since it had been a wet summer, and they could see the fields around the house in the valley a little distance away.

She spread a blanket and began to get the food out of the containers Ronan brought from the truck. He had a real thing about women carrying anything heavy, she thought. If she so much as got close to the cooler, he was there, asking her where she wanted it.

It was nearly seven o'clock when they all sat down on the blanket to eat. She'd prepared fried chicken as well as baked beans, which she'd kept hot in an insulated casserole dish, and a seven-layer salad with peas in it so she could get some vegetables into her sons, who thought cows and rabbits were the only creatures who should eat green stuff. She'd also brought some silly, molded gelatin shapes for the boys, their favorite no-bake chocolate cookies, potato chips and Ronan's watermelon.

It seemed to take only moments for the three males to demolish all the food. She'd delayed as long as she could so that she wouldn't be stuck sitting out there with Ronan for hours waiting for the fireworks to start, but the boys weren't used to eating late, and she could only wait so long. They still had more than two hours until dark, when the fireworks display would begin.

The boys scampered off to investigate a hole Tommy

had discovered in the ground, convinced there must be a giant groundhog inside.

"That was delicious," Ronan said as he picked up the paper plates and dumped them in a plastic trash bag she'd brought. "Thanks for letting me come along. I know it wasn't your idea."

She smiled, a quick and impersonal expression. She hoped. "The boys are enjoying having you with us."

"But you're not."

"I'm enjoying seeing Lee and Tommy harass someone else for a little while." She was going to keep this neighborly and friendly, casual, if it killed her.

He smiled, but he didn't rise to the change of subject. "Deirdre."

"Yes?"

"I want to apologize—"

"That's not necessary. I don't want to talk about it." She turned away so fast her braid almost hit her in the mouth. Grabbing the thick hank of hair, she slung it over her shoulder with more force than she needed.

"It is necessary," Ronan said. His voice was quiet, but she recognized the same hint of steel she'd heard when he said he would carry the cooler. "I'm sorry if I made a wrong assumption that night. Maybe I believed what I wanted to believe."

She turned back to him, desperate to get him to stop talking, and found he was right behind her. "It's okay. We made a mistake."

He was gazing down into her eyes. "Are you sure?"

"I'm not sure of anything right now." She had ceased to care whether or not he heard the note of desperation in her voice. "Can't we just forget it?"

"I can't." He lifted his hand, and as if she were underwater, in slow-as-molasses motion, she watched it come toward her, then she felt the rough drag of his finger along her bottom lip. "Can you?"

He was too close; she wanted to back away, but her body had other ideas and her feet were rooted to the ground as she fought not to simply melt against him. "No," she admitted in a muted tone, closing her eyes.

"I told you I was sorry about misunderstanding you, but I'm not sorry about what happened." The finger probed gently along the sensitive inner flesh of her lip, causing fresh desire to heat her blood. His voice dropped even lower. "I think about it all the time. About the little noises you made, about how soft the skin on the underside of your breasts was, about the way you felt around me."

She couldn't draw breath, so thick was the air around her. "Stop it." Her voice was a hoarse plea.

He smiled, a knowing, dangerous smile. "I want to make love to you again. But this time I want to carry you to a bed. I want to have hours and hours to taste every inch of you. I want to feel your hands touching me. Anywhere you like."

He withdrew his finger from her mouth and slid his hand around the back of her neck, seizing her braid and tugging until her face was tilted up to him. "Tell me you want me, too."

His mouth was a breath away from hers; if she lifted herself on tiptoe, he'd be kissing her. His hand lay against the back of her neck, and she could feel the heat of his big body only inches away. A surge of feeling, strong and sure, rushed through her. "I want you, too."

His lips descended. But unlike last time, he made love to her mouth alone, ravishing every inch, nipping at her bottom lip and licking a soothing comfort on the small sting. His tongue sought hers, enticed her to play, then plunged deep, claiming her surrender. In her abdomen, a seductive, throbbing ache began and she closed her eyes, giving herself to sensation.

Then, as she was on the verge of pressing herself against him, encircling his wide shoulders with her arms and offering herself to any whim he had, he ended the kiss, retreating slowly until his lips were barely touching hers. The grasp on her hair relaxed. He began to withdraw his hand and as he did so, he deliberately allowed it to trail over her shoulder, the fingers slipping down the slope of her breast to briefly brush one sensitive tip before moving away. She gasped, and her body jerked in an involuntary sexual reaction to that touch.

He chuckled, low in his throat.

She opened her eyes, seeing only Ronan filling her view. He was smiling, though deep in his eyes lurked a hot, dark, wanting that echoed in her blood. "That was a start."

"Ronan!" It was the shrill voice of her youngest child. "Come play ball wif us!"

"Reality has really bad timing." He grinned. The sexual intent faded from his eyes, but before he turned to jog off across the meadow to where her boys waited, he stopped and gave her a long, serious look. "Don't even think about pretending this didn't happen."

While Ronan played catch with her sons, Deirdre finished packing away the picnic supplies, except for the cookies and a big batch of green grapes she'd brought for munching on later. So many thoughts swirled around in her head that she finally sat down on the blanket with her knees drawn up and her arms wrapped around them, giving her full attention to sorting out the crazy feelings she was experiencing.

And they really were crazy, she thought. She knew next to nothing about Ronan except that with one kiss he could have her ready to roll over and beg for his touch. She had only known him for a matter of weeks, and for more than half of that they'd barely been speaking. How could you love someone with whom you had never spent a day, never gone out on a date, never even held hands on a front porch or kissed on the stoop?

But what they had done on her porch certainly made up for it.

She groaned, resting her forehead on her knees. She'd been young and stupid, easily blinded the first time she'd fallen in love, and it had turned out to be only a thin veneer that quickly began to show wear. She'd promised herself she'd be sensible, take her time, get to know a man before leaping into another relationship.

Right.

Here she was, falling in love with a man whose birth date and middle name she didn't even know. The only thing about him she was sure of was that when he touched her, her world felt so right she knew she finally understood what she'd been missing before. He was so beautifully made and so handsome to her that she couldn't take her eyes off him. Ronan came charging through the field toward her as she watched, with one little boy held upside down under each arm. Each child was screaming madly and giggling—and her heart broke its final thread-thin moorings and flew straight off to the man of her dreams.

As it turned out, they didn't even get the lawn chairs out of the Bronco. As the light began to fade from the sky, Ronan brought out his bag of tricks. Deirdre had never seen her children so excited.

Or so obedient. He told them firmly that they had to sit in one place while he lit the fuses on the "snakes," the "cherry bombs" and the "pinwheels" in a bare spot down near the stream. If either of them disobeyed, he warned them, he would put the fireworks away. For good.

Why did they believe him? If she'd said that, sure as the sun rose, one or the other would be sneaking around behind her trying to get a better look.

He amused them with the small fireworks for a while, then got out the box of sparklers. He stood with Lee, while she kept a cautious hand over Tommy's as they pierced the air with the sizzling sticks. They repeated it several times until the box was empty, and by then it was fully dark.

"Let's get comfortable on the blanket," she said to the boys. "The town fireworks will be starting soon." They bounced over to where she indicated, but it was apparent that little eyes were growing weary, and they didn't argue when she suggested the view might be better if they were lying flat. Ronan had been standing silently while she settled her children; as she rose, she said to him, "If we get the chairs from the back of the Bronco, we can sit right here behind them."

"I have a better idea." He took her wrist and drew her down onto the blanket. Sitting with his back propped against the tree, he drew her between his bent knees. "Lean back," he said.

She let him draw her close but she suddenly felt self-conscious, sitting in his embrace in front of her children. Just then, the first beautiful display lit the sky in a blossoming burst of pink and gold.

"Look, Mom!" Lee cast her one unconcerned glance as he pointed toward the sky. "Look up or you'll miss 'em."

She did, and Ronan used the opportunity to gently pull her toward him so that her back was against his chest and her head rested against one shoulder. He was warm, and hard, and he smelled so wonderfully of clean male animal that she couldn't resist the urge to linger for a moment. Then his arms snaked beneath hers and linked across her waist, and the sensation of being protected, cared for and coddled, was too much to resist. Her body relaxed; she laid her arms over the whipcord strength of his forearms and savored the moment.

The fireworks display lasted nearly an hour. She, "Oohed," and, "Aahed," with the boys but after a while, she noticed their voices fading into sleepy mumbles. Ronan pushed himself to his feet at one point, and when she made to follow him, he shook his head.

"I'll lay them on the back seat of the truck. If they stay there much longer, they're going to get bitten by a million mosquitoes."

He was right, but what amazed her was that he thought of it at all.

When the boys were safely, and soundly, he assured her, sleeping in the Bronco, he returned to the blanket and eased himself down behind her exactly as he had been before. It felt so right it was scary. For once, she decided, she would agonize and worry in the morning. Right now, all she was going to do was enjoy the companionship and closeness, snuggled in the dark under a spangled, flashing sky.

Finally the fireworks display ended. There was no reason to linger any longer, no reason at all. She really should move. But it was hard to convince her body, snuggled into the warm circle of his arms. Turning her head, she said, "Thank you for joining us tonight. You made this a memorable Fourth for Tommy and Lee."

"And how about their mother?" His jawbone was just at the level of her ear; he turned his head and placed his lips against her temple.

She smiled, unable to squelch the tentative tide of happiness rising in her heart. "For their mother, too," she admitted.

"Good." His voice sounded as if it rumbled up from a very deep well. He lifted his hand, putting a finger beneath her chin and tilting her face back and up as he lowered his head and sought her lips.

Her breath shuddered out on a wave of pure, unadulterated desire. Butterflies took wing in her stomach, quickly moving lower to flutter tantalizingly in her womb.

He kissed her as he had earlier, learning every nook and cranny of her mouth, drinking her response with his tongue, tracing the outline of her mouth and encouraging her to explore him as thoroughly. He taught her how erotic an ear could be, using his tongue again in combination with gentle sucklings that had her sighing aloud as she shifted against him.

His hands flattened against her body. One moved up to bracket a breast, worrying the nipple with a rhythmic brush as his other hand moved lower, spreading over her stomach, moving even lower to trace the seam of her jeans, the seam that was as hot as the steaming center of her.

She was beyond protest, beyond thinking of anything except the hands molding, stroking, petting her body. One moved between her legs, cupping her most private parts in his strong hand, and the pressure of his mouth suddenly became wild and hot, untamed and unyielding.

He groaned, and she realized her hips were moving, circling in response to the stroke and press of his hand. She could feel him, erect and rock solid against her back. The flesh between her legs felt as if it were the collection point of sensation in her body, the seal of his mouth on hers and his hand on her breast shooting straight to her hot, throbbing center. She felt herself softening, knew that beneath the jeans she was wet, and he knew it, too.

His hand withdrew from between her legs and she cried out, a cry stifled by his mouth as he deftly unbuttoned and unzipped her pants in one smooth motion. Shocking in its suddenness, she felt his palm against her bared belly, sliding beneath her panties and spearing down to rest in its previous spot, unhindered by fabric. His fingers were rough against her tenderness, quickly dewed with moisture. One bold digit traced the long fold that hid her feminine secrets, inexorably pushing up into her, and she felt her body gather in one great strand of tension that burst with one final press of his hidden finger upward inside her soft flesh.

Deirdre heaved and shuddered in his arms, her hands clenched so tightly on his thighs that he knew he would carry small finger marks for a few days. As the final spasms of her pleasure receded and her body went limp in his arms, he slowly withdrew his hand from the soft, slick passage. He kissed her mouth one final time, holding on to his own control by the merest thread.

"We have to stop." His body shook with the effort it took not to simply lie back with her in his arms and roll so that he could cover her. He was so hard he hurt within the cramped confines of the jeans he'd worn, and the gentle pressure of her butt as she wriggled against him made him grit his teeth and groan.

"Aren't you going to take a turn?"

The teasing question broke his control, sent blind staggering need driving through him, focusing everything within him on relieving the building pressure. He hesitated, but even in his maddened state, he remembered that her children were sleeping not fifty yards away in the truck.

Abruptly he surged to his feet, dragging her with him to the far side of the huge old oak tree. His hand shook as he tore open his pants, but he froze as he realized he didn't have anything with him. He couldn't. They couldn't. Taking a second chance would be akin to spitting in the eye of Fate.

"We can't." It was a growl of desperate disappointment. "I didn't bring anything with me."

He started to turn away from her, but she stopped him simply by sliding one palm into his briefs and grasping his distended flesh. He gasped at the hot ecstasy that her small fingers offered. Her hand slipped lower, and the feel of her fingers on him nearly blew off the top of his head. She lifted him free, and tentatively began to stroke him. Surrendering all control, he placed his hand over hers and guided her into a tighter grip, a faster rhythm. The stroke of her soft palm was more than he could take, not nearly what he needed, but all that he could allow. With an agonized groan, his back arched and he gave himself to the primitive instincts. His hips pumped again and again and again in counterpoint to her motion; he felt his flesh grow-

ing larger, tauter, than he'd ever experienced. Finally, after
a wild, reckless speeding journey into the fires of sensual
immersion, he poured his hot, slippery essence into her
waiting hands, his body jerking as he gasped and groaned
in time to his release.

As the spasms slowly abated, he slumped against the
tree, shaking, one arm thrown across his eyes. She released
him, and he started when her palm touched the tip of his
still-engorged flesh as she slipped away. He heard her rus-
tling around, but he stayed where he was, knowing that his
legs wouldn't support him if he stepped away from the tree.

She was back in a minute, and to his relief, she came to
his side, slipping one arm around his waist and leaning into
him in silence. His strength was returning and he used the
napkin she offered him, then eased his cooling flesh into
his briefs. He turned, drawing her into his arms, holding
her against his heart and knowing that whatever happened,
he would never be the same.

Great sex? Unquestionably. Each time with her was the
best he'd ever had, and the best he knew he was ever going
to experience in this lifetime. But she meant more to him
than that, and he was just discovering how important it was
to hold on to her, to bind her to him so closely that she
forgot any other man, to make a place for himself in her
warm, loving heart, a permanent place.

But he'd rushed her again, drawn her into the sensual
whirlpool they'd created, without giving her a chance to
decide whether or not she was ready for him. Had he mis-
read her signals? The same uneasiness that had gripped him
after the first time he'd made love to her surfaced, and he
forced himself to speak, dreading her response.

"If another apology is in order, let me make it now. I
really didn't intend for this to get out of hand—"

She giggled.

He stopped, realized why she was amused, and reluctantly his own sense of humor kicked in. "Very funny."

She lifted her arms and put them around his neck, linking them and leaning back to look into his face. In the moonlight he could see her green cat eyes crinkled in laughter, but as he watched she slowly sobered. "Ronan—" she hesitated "—you don't have any apologies to make." Her eyelids lowered, and he realized she was embarrassed. "I've never behaved this way in my whole life. It's like you're a giant, walking aphrodisiac—one whiff and I'm senseless."

He grinned as a relief so intense it almost hurt burned through his veins. "A walking aphrodisiac, huh? Not a bad description of what you do to me, either." He rocked her gently back and forth, lifting her off her feet and swinging her playfully in his arms. "What are we going to do about it?"

She looked up at him, a question in her eyes. "I...I don't know." Something fragile and frightened crossed her face. "This is moving so fast I can't even believe it's happened."

"Believe it, baby." He kissed her, gently invading her mouth until she was clinging to him again, bent backward against his arm in total surrender. "We can take it a day at a time if that makes you more comfortable." He paused, then decided there was no point in dissembling. "But from now on, you're private property. Trespassers will be shot on sight."

He'd intended the words to be lightly uttered, tossed off easily, a jesting way of letting her know he was staking a claim. But he couldn't pull it off, and his voice was clipped and final.

She searched his face for a moment, and he held his breath, wondering if she was about to beat him over the head for acting like a caveman. For presuming too much.

Then she leaned forward, pressing a gentle kiss to the hollow of his throat where his pulse surged. "Okay."

They stood in silence for a moment, then he took her

arms from around his neck. He closed her jeans and then his, wistfully wishing he had time, privacy and protection, so that he could do what he wanted, so that he could pull her into his arms after he'd loved her to exhaustion, so that he could wake with her in the same embrace the next morning. "Come on, Sleeping Beauty, time to take those kids home."

"I'm not sleeping," she pointed out. He rolled the blanket into an untidy heap and they got in the Bronco, Ronan at the wheel for the drive back down to the house.

"Maybe not," he said. "But when I kiss you, you awaken in a very big way." She didn't say anything, and he reached over and took her hand. "Now what? I can hear you thinking."

"Nothing. I wasn't thinking, I was blushing."

He chuckled. "Not used to a man being so frank?"

"Not used to a man at all." There was the beginning of a troubled note in her voice and he was glad they were almost back to the house. He needed to get her back in his arms, where she could forget everything she'd learned from that crummy ex-husband of hers, where he could teach her how it was going to be with them.

At the house, they had a brief, whispered argument when she picked up Tommy after he'd lifted Lee out of the Bronco. He didn't want her carrying anything, hurting herself in any way. It might be unreasonable, but he didn't care. She was too fragile, too small and delicate to be carrying a three-year-old around. "He's too heavy for you."

"He is not. I carry him all the time."

"Let me have him. You can open doors."

She shot him an exasperated look that found its mark, even in the little light the one spotlight on the stable produced. "He only weighs thirty-five pounds. I can carry him." She turned and walked toward the house.

He followed, preparing to argue some more, when Lee stirred on his shoulder. The little boy drew back, frowning.

Then the small body relaxed, little arms coming up to clutch over his shoulders. "Ronan." It was nothing more than a sleepy mutter, the sound full of the satisfaction that comes with security. Lee turned his head into the curve of Ronan's neck, asleep again, his breath gusting warm against Ronan's skin.

It pierced his heart with a pain so sharp he stopped in his tracks.

God, he adored these little kids. They were feisty and ornery, and into something every second you looked away, but he wouldn't trade them for all the other kids in the world. The realization was a forceful blow, and a staggering idea lanced through his head. *If he married Deirdre, he could have them all.* These two could be *his* boys, and the woman stepping through the door ahead of him, the woman he wanted so badly that he ached with it, could be *his* woman. His to share a bed with every night, his to chuckle with at the boys' antics, his to celebrate with when another book went *New York Times* bestseller.

But she thinks you're a...a less-successful writer. He winced inwardly. He'd told her that initially, purely out of habit, self-preservation, whatever. But he still hadn't told her the truth, and he knew instinctively that Deirdre would have a hard time accepting his reasons for the lie.

And they were good ones, he assured himself. Privacy was a big issue in his life, and not just because he enjoyed it. The security firm he'd engaged after the stalking incident had taught him some hard-and-fast rules that celebrities who wanted to live safely followed. When he'd first rented the apartment, he hadn't known whether or not he could trust Deirdre to preserve his privacy.

And then there was the personal side of it. He'd fallen for a woman whose heart had loved his pocketbook more than him, once, and she'd walked away with damn near half his assets. He might not have loved Sonja the way he should have, but it had cut at his pride to find out how she'd used him. He didn't intend to give another female that chance. The women he met in his public persona were kept at a distance; if he ever found a woman he wanted, he didn't want to wonder whether she wanted him or his millions.

A woman he wanted. Well, he'd found her.

He'd tell her tomorrow, he promised himself. He'd do it tonight, except that he knew she was tired; he'd caught her yawning behind her hand on the trip back down to the house. She would understand why he'd lied.

Why he'd misled her, he corrected himself. It wasn't as if he'd deliberately set out to hide who he was from her. How was he to know she was going to sneak into his life and clear out the empty spaces, filling them with herself and her sons?

Five

"**H**ow could it be Sunday already? I swear, since this visitation arrangement started, Sundays roll around faster than once a week," Deirdre grumbled as she packed a little bag for her sons to take on their weekly visit with their father. "Whoever is in charge of the days of the week added a few extra Sundays into the old seven-day schedule, I just know it."

Ronan grinned as he lounged in the doorway watching her. The boys had led him to her a moment ago and promptly vanished again. But they hadn't gone far; he could hear giggling, so he tamped down the urge to walk over and pull her into his arms for the kind of greeting he really wanted to give her.

But it was just as well. She was tense and distracted, and he could see the anxiety in her eyes. When he'd asked her if she and the boys would like to go to the Inner Harbor with him on Sunday, she'd explained the situation with her ex-husband. He'd volunteered to go with her to drop the boys off and told her they could drive down just for a few hours until time for the kids to return.

"Are you guys ready to go?"

"Yes, Mom." Both boys appeared and scampered out to the Bronco, whooping with glee when they learned they were going to get to ride in Ronan's truck.

They buckled the boys together in one seat belt between them, and he drove into Baltimore, following her directions to her friend Frannie's house. On the way, she told him that Frannie had a business designing custom bridal gowns. As they turned onto her street, Deirdre pointed out the sign that read, "Brooks' Bridals." The place was a pretty, brick two-story, and she directed him around the corner to another entrance, which turned out to be the family's front door.

They were a few minutes early, he noted, but her ex-husband was already there, sitting in his car, smoking a cigarette as he waited. He knew who it was because Tommy said, "There's Daddy," in a surprisingly subdued tone. As they drove up, "Daddy" tossed a smoldering cigarette butt into the street. *Charming example for your kids. Jerk.*

He noticed Deirdre's mouth tighten, but she didn't even look at him as they pulled into the driveway.

The door of the brick house opened. A big man emerged, striding down the driveway. "That's Jack," Deirdre said. Jack had a puzzled look on his face at the unfamiliar truck, but as he got near enough to see Deirdre, the expression changed to a wide grin. Ronan didn't miss the cool glance aimed his way.

Hmm. Were the hackles raised on Deirdre's behalf or was there just something about his face the guy didn't like? Fine. Ronan didn't particularly like him, either, when he swung Deirdre out of the truck for a big, far-too-close hug that lasted far too long, in his critical eyes, before turning to lift down the boys.

Ronan got out and walked around to stand at Deirdre's side. She had tears in her eyes as she held each son close for an instant before saying goodbye. To his surprise Lee turned to him with his arms held high in a clear demand that his little brother echoed instantly.

Ronan bent and scooped a child into each arm. "Be good," he ordered. "Have fun. But don't have too much fun without me." The boys were giggling, and they threw their arms around his neck, hugging hard before he set them down. As Jack took each of them by the hand, Ronan realized that his throat was tight.

His stomach hardened into a cold lump of lead as he watched this ritual that she went through every week, and he didn't find her comments about extra Sundays very funny anymore. She sniffled, and he put an arm around her shoulders as the car drove away, pulling her into his arms. "They'll be back in just a few hours," he soothed, stroking his hand up and down her back.

"I know." Her voice was forlorn as she laid her head against his chest. Then she squared her shoulders and lifted her chin, stepping out of his arms. She smiled at the guy walking back toward them. "Jack," she called, "I want you to meet Ronan. Frannie already met him a few weeks ago."

"I heard." Jack came forward and stuck out an enormous, meaty paw. "Jack Ferris."

Ronan took it, knowing he'd better make his first statement with his grip. His hand met Jack's, and they firmly clasped hands, each increasing the pressure. "Ronan Sullivan."

Jack nodded, unsmiling. He was tall and broad shouldered, but Ronan doubted there was an ounce of fat on him. His hair was so short Ronan wondered if he'd been military. The handshake lasted for another moment. Then, with a final shake that declared a standoff, they mutually relaxed the pressure and withdrew their hands.

"Come on in," Jack said, "Frannie's inside with the midgets."

"All right, but only for a minute." Deirdre started forward, darting a smile at Ronan. "We're going down to the Inner Harbor for a few hours."

The inside of the house was decorated with comfortable, homey-looking furniture. A liberal dusting of children's toys coated every surface, and Deirdre's friend Frannie was just coming down the stairs. Although she was several inches taller than Deirdre, she wasn't exceptionally tall. But she gave the impression of height, probably because of her slender build and long, slim legs.

Frannie had the baby he'd seen before—Brooks—in one arm, and with the other, she held the hand of a tiny blond child who was carefully stepping down, setting both feet on each step before approaching the next. The little girl squealed loudly when she saw Deirdre.

"Hi," Frannie called. "Please ignore the mess. I was going to do the Cleanup Shuffle before you got here, but Brooks foiled my plans with one of his own." She smiled ruefully at her husband. "If he'd waited ten more minutes, Jack could have had the pleasure of changing him."

As they reached the bottom, Jack stepped around Deirdre and took Brooks from his wife's arms. "Good boy," he said to the infant. "Your timing was perfect."

"Hello, Ronan," Frannie said, and he saw that her eyes were as cool and wary as her husband's. "I didn't expect to see you again."

Ah, that was it. The last time they'd met, things had been…tense, between Deirdre and him. Obviously there had been some girl talk going on. And he'd bet his belt that Frannie had told her husband.

He smiled at her. "Ditto. But here I am."

"Um, Ronan and I are going down to the harbor for a while," Deirdre said. "We probably won't be back much

before seven, so don't worry about feeding us dinner.''
Seven was the hour the boys were returned.

"Are you sure?" Frannie asked. "You know it's no trouble, and it would give us a chance to visit with Ronan.''

Was it his imagination, or was there a meaningful tone
in her invitation? He couldn't think of many things less
appealing than "visiting" with Deirdre's disapproving
friend and the hulking guy eyeing him from the easy chair,
and when Deirdre said, "I'm sure. Another time, I promise,'' he was relieved. Besides, he didn't want to share a
moment of the few hours he would have alone with her.

They drove to the Inner Harbor, parking in a deck across
the street from the Pratt Street pavilion of shops and eat-
eries that abutted the wide, brick-lined walkways along the
water's edge. Couples sat in the shade of umbrellas and
canopies on the decks of restaurants; parents kept an eagle
eye on children fascinated by the lapping water in the harbor only steps away below the sea wall. Tourists streamed
toward the Maryland Science Center at one end and the
Baltimore Aquarium at the other, some stopping to shop
and to check out the old submarine permanently on display,
while others rented tiny paddleboats and took an hour's
leisure in the harbor waters. Small cruise boats loaded
streams of people, while in the small stone amphitheatre, a
juggler was putting on a show with a variety of unusual
items. The air was filled with bouncy Slavic tunes from the
ethnic festival, which, from the sound of it, must have been
displaying the culture of the Ukraine, Hungary or some
other Eastern European people this week.

He pulled her into the shopping pavilion for Italian ices,
which they ate as they window-shopped. She passed dis-
plays of trendy clothing and glittering gems without a
whimper, but when they came to a toy store, Deirdre all
but pressed her nose to the glass.

"Look!" she said in delight. In the window, an enormous contraption had been built with plastic pieces of pipe

and other similar attachments that clearly came from a building kit of some kind. As they watched, a clerk dropped a marble into the chute at the top of the setup. The marble wound its way down through myriad obstacles, circling madly down a funnel-shaped cone, plopping onto the end of a springboard, which triggered the descent of a second marble, zigzagging this way and that until finally it reached the bottom.

"Wouldn't the boys love that!" she exclaimed.

Ronan grinned. "I'd be willing to bet they'd make some interesting modifications to it."

She nodded ruefully. "Almost makes you want to pity the marbles."

He linked his fingers with hers. "Come on. Let's go in and get it."

But to his surprise she dug in her heels and resisted. "No. Lee and Tommy don't really need a new toy."

"Oh, come on," he said, tugging at her hand. "They'd love this thing. You'll be sorry if we leave here without it."

He passed an arm around her back to escort her into the store, but still she resisted, making her body stiff and shaking her head. "No!" she repeated in a soft, but determined, undertone. "I can't afford to spend money on toys right now, Ronan."

"No problem," he said. "I'll buy it."

Impatiently she tossed her braid over her shoulder. "You don't have to buy my children presents," she said. "They like you already."

"How about their mother?" He shifted, pushing her to the edge of the throng of summer shoppers, against the glass of the toy store window. "Does she like me, too?"

Her lashes came down, veiling her expressive eyes. "As if you need to be told," she said.

"Then why not let me buy your children a little gift? It's no big deal."

"It is a big deal," she insisted. "I'll buy the boys new toys when I can afford it. But I refuse to accept that kind of gift."

Well, hell. Why was she being so stubborn? It wasn't like it was going to bankrupt him—although she didn't know that yet. And he certainly wasn't about to explain it to her here. "All right," he said. "You win. Do I have permission to buy them each one of those bug-catching kits?"

Pressed against her as he was, he could feel the moment her body relaxed. "You do," she said, giving him a smile that made her dimples flash and made him want to drop his head and cover her lush lips with his own. "They'd enjoy those, I'm sure."

A short while later she dragged him down to where the water taxis docked. "I want to take you over to Fells' Point. There's a really great little place to eat."

He wanted to take *her* to the nearest hotel room, a tantalizing few steps away in the Stouffer's Renaissance above another pavilion of shops, and spend the afternoon slaking his never-ending desire for her in the coolness of an air-conditioned room. In a bed. That would be a novel experience.

But he dragged his thoughts away from the delightful contemplation. He was getting damn tired of this permanent hard-on. He needed to give Deirdre a chance to get used to him, to learn to know him well enough to trust him when he explained about his career. And then he could ask her to marry him.

He hadn't thought marriage would work for him—until he'd met Deirdre. It certainly hadn't worked the first time. Sonja hadn't understood his need for solitary hours to create. Deirdre was the kind of woman who would understand the weird ritual of closing himself away every day to sweat out a few pages of print. Sonja had thrown fits when he didn't want to go out and "be seen" in all the hot spots;

she'd nearly driven him insane trying to get him to agree to move to L.A. Translation: Hollywood.

Deirdre was different. She was family oriented; she was calm. She was industrious and busy with her own little business. And she was more exciting to him every minute he spent with her.

Marriage would allow him access to those sweet, soft curves every night. He could fall asleep with those warm ivory breasts pressed against him and wake her up in various appealing ways— *Enough's enough, you idiot!* he reminded himself as the water taxi pulled in to the pier.

They sat in the sun at the prow of the little boat, laughing when salty spray from the small wavelets they rode came up to dampen their skin and clothing. Deirdre took him to the restaurant, a chic little French place where they had their turn being one of the couples under the umbrellas.

Couple. He liked the sound of that word, when it applied to Deirdre and him. He'd never felt like part of a couple before, not even during the three short years of his marriage. He wondered if Deirdre had ever felt that way. "Tell me about your marriage," he said over the crusty bread and wine they were sharing.

She obviously was startled. "Why?" she asked bluntly.

He thought about it a minute. "You must have thought the guy was nice enough at one time. You wouldn't have married him if you'd known what he was really like. When did he change?"

"I don't think he ever changed," she said slowly. "He worked for Bethlehem Steel, and I got my first job out of college there. He was handsome and attentive, and pretty overwhelming to a lowly assistant in the sales division. I have a degree in business administration. Bet you didn't know that!" She smiled, and he was dazzled by the momentary flash of genuine amusement. God, she was beautiful when she was happy.

The grin faded as she toyed with her fork, and after a

moment, she spoke again. "He swept me off my feet. I was flattered by the interest of a company executive—even then, Nelson was one of the golden boys. I think I was in love with the idea of love. My parents have been married, very happily, for more than thirty years, and it never occurred to me that there was any other kind of marriage."

She never should have had to learn it, either. "So how long was it before you realized he wasn't the guy you thought he was?"

Again she smiled, but this time there was no humor in it, only self-condemnation. "About two weeks. The day before we came back from our honeymoon, I caught him with a woman he'd met in the hotel bar."

He was shocked, and unreasonably furious, considering all this was old news and he hadn't even known her then. Bastard. "So why didn't—"

"He convinced me that it was never going to happen again," she said. "And I believed him. And a few weeks later I found out I was pregnant." Suddenly she looked weary. "After that, I pretended everything was fine for a while. And *pretend* is the only word for it. Nobody could find him when I went into labor. My mother was with me when Lee was born." She stopped and took a sip of wine, looking pensively out over the harbor. "I should have called it quits then, I know. I even knew it in my heart. But the thought of my little boy growing up without a father…"

She swallowed. "I'm a real ass," she said glumly.

"No, you're not." He reached for her hands and held them in his on the table. "You're a great mother, and you wanted to do what was best for your child."

"Well, I finally acknowledged that I had a lousy marriage and an even lousier husband," she said. "But not soon enough. By the time Lee was six months old, Nelson wasn't even trying to hide the affairs. But if he even thought I had looked at another man, it sent him into a blue fit. I think he thought of me as property," she added. "I got pregnant with Tommy the night he thought I had come on to his boss at a company picnic. He held me down," she said baldly. She looked away again, and he saw that her eyes were filled with tears.

Gently he stroked his thumbs over the backs of her palms. His stomach roiled. Given what she'd been through in that marriage, it was amazing that she'd ever let him touch her, he thought, much less participate in the moments of wild, hot lovemaking that seemed to take over common sense every time they were alone. "You deserve better," he said quietly, rage a bitter taste in his throat.

"I finally figured that out." She removed her hands from his and picked up a napkin, dabbing at her eyes. "Sorry. It's humiliating to have been so gullible, and even more humiliating to remember how long I tolerated it."

He shook his head. He'd heard about it before, had written about it as well. He could understand the motivation behind wanting to hold on. "It sounds terrible," he said. "I admire you for getting out when you did. Raising those two little hellions alone can't be easy, but you make it look like it is."

She smiled, and he realized she'd heard the affection in his voice. "It has its moments," she said in wry understatement, "but I'm used to it. I raised them alone even when I was married."

"How long have you been divorced?"

"It was two years in March. But I think of it as three years, since that's when I left him."

He thought back. "You must have separated shortly after we met at that Christmas party."

She blushed. From her long white neck to her hairline where the black curls began, her face turned a bright scarlet. She moaned and hid her face in her hands.

"What?" He was amused, and curious about what he'd

said that possibly could have produced that kind of reaction.

She lowered her hands. "I left Nelson in early March, when Tommy was a month old. And it was thanks to you."

"To me?"

She nodded. "You were so kind that night, making sure I wasn't left sitting alone, that I had a way home.... All I could think was that if I were single—and smaller than a water buffalo—I would have been free to dance with this incredibly attractive man, to flirt, maybe to accept a date." Her face was still red. "Oh, I knew you were there with someone else, but—"

"She was my cousin," he said. "And it's a good thing I didn't know what you were thinking, because I spent the whole evening thinking that you were the most beautiful thing I'd ever seen and wishing I was the one with the right to take you home." Beneath the tiny table, he had his long legs stretched out on either side of hers. Now he closed them, gently pressing against the outsides of her knees with his own, then shifting to insert one thigh between her legs, telling her without words what he was thinking now.

He looked across the table at her face, and it was all he could do not to drag her out of her seat onto his lap and kiss her senseless. Her eyes had gone soft and wide, slightly unfocused as she stared at his mouth. Her pretty lips were parted just the slightest bit, and he could see her breasts rise and fall as her breathing increased.

"Stop looking at me like that," he said, knowing his voice was deep, as aroused as the rest of him. "Or I'll forget the good intentions I had, and we'll head back across the harbor and I'll have you under me in a bed faster than you can say please."

The corners of her lips tilted up. Beneath the table, her legs rubbed up and down against his thigh the slightest bit, but enough to raise his blood pressure another notch. "Please," she said in a soft, teasing voice.

A rush of purely sexual anticipation brought him to his feet. He reached for his wallet and withdrew a bill large enough to cover a generous tip. Tossing it onto the table, he circled her wrist with one hand, pulling her to her feet. Without saying a word, he escorted her from the restaurant. The moment they were out on the sidewalk, he turned and dragged her into his arms, holding her against him while he took her mouth in a deep, searching kiss until they were both gasping for breath. He could feel her breasts rising and falling; she was breathing almost as heavily as he.

"Come on." He took her hand and pulled her back up the street to the taxi dock. They didn't speak. He simply stood behind her with his hands linked across her stomach as he had the night of the fireworks, a position that pressed him intimately against her. On the trip across the bay, he held her on his lap. The trip seemed to last forever. The minute his feet hit solid ground, he headed for the hotel he'd noted earlier.

The room was a standard hotel room. He didn't open the drapes, just tore the bedspread back to the foot of the king-size bed before he came back to her. She was standing in the middle of the room, waiting for him, and she stood quietly while he removed every item of clothing she wore and tossed it across a nearby chair. He got rid of his nearly as fast.

When he turned back to her, she moved to come into his arms but he stopped her. "I want to look at you," he said. "I want to see your body, so that the next time we're groping each other in a field or a closet or the floor of the stable, I'll know what I'm touching, even if I haven't had time to get all your clothes off."

She was blushing again, but she continued to stand there, arms at her sides, letting him look his fill. He raised one hand to her throat, circling the slender column, then took the elastic band from the end of her braid and combed his fingers through it, creating a wild mass of curls that he spread over her shoulders before letting his hand slide down to cover one breast. He'd been right, he saw. Pink nipples, light against the lovely fullness of her flesh. He bent and took one into his mouth, suckling her strongly, and she made a small sound of pleasure. Going down on one knee, he reached around to palm her buttocks and pull her forward, laying his head against her soft belly. He took a moment to appreciate the gentle scent of woman as he turned his head and pressed kisses across the tender skin.

He slipped one hand between her thighs, urging her to widen her stance, nuzzling the fine soft nest of black curls at the junction of her legs. Her docility was as arousing as the wild way she had given herself to him in the past, and he curled his tongue, pressing between the curls, seeking the softer flesh hidden beneath. She whimpered and opened her legs a bit more, pushing her hips at him, and he felt his own stiffened flesh leap in response.

Rising, he urged her the few steps to the bed, laying her across the white sheets before coming down beside her propped on his elbow, one hand on her belly. "This time," he said, "I'm prepared." Rolling away, he snagged his pants and found his wallet, withdrawing a small, flat package that he tore open unceremoniously. He was throbbing, hard and hot for her, and he didn't want to wait another minute. He sat back on his knees, but as he began the process of slipping on the soft latex, she came up beside him. Her hands brushed his out of the way, and he sat back on his heels and let her gently stroke the barrier into place. He let his head drop back, unable to watch her work on him, succumbing to the delicious sensation of her small hands, until she was finally finished and she placed her hands at his hips.

"Please," she said, as before.

And as before, that one little word had the power to totally destroy his senses. He pulled her down again and came to her, his pulsing shaft pressed against her, and she wriggled her hips in an invitation that he didn't hesitate to accept. He used his hand to open a place for himself, knowing she could take him when he felt the soft, dewy flesh slick beneath his fingertips. Slowly, he pulled back, guiding himself to the entrance of the feminine passage, then just as slowly pushed forward, sliding into her on one long glide that ended only when they were pressed together body to body, his hardness solidly ensconced within her.

She put her hands to his shoulders, looking up at him, trusting him totally, and he dropped his head and kissed her, keeping it soft and gentle. He'd never felt this before, this tenderness that mixed with the lust he felt for her pretty body, turning it into something deeper, something he never wanted to lose. He put his hands to each side of her face, looking deeply into her eyes, and began to thrust slowly in and out of her.

"Do you know what you do to me?" he asked her.

"The same thing that you do to me," she said, smiling a little. Then, to his dismay, tears welled in her eyes.

He stopped moving. "Baby, what's wrong?"

"I'm sorry." She tried to smile but it turned into an adorable quiver of her chin. "This is just so...so..."

"So what?" He could hear the alarm in his own voice.

"So...wonderful."

"I know," he said in relief. He stroked away the tracks of the tears that slid back into her thick hair. "It's never been like this for me, either." They stayed locked together in silent contemplation for a moment. But his body wouldn't let him stay still for long, and he began moving his hips forward and back again, need mounting as she raised her legs and ran the soles of her feet down the backs of his calves.

He slipped his hands beneath her thighs and pulled her legs up around his waist, and she locked her ankles behind his back as he increased the rhythm of his motion. She was rocking beneath him, small cries of pleasure slipping from her throat with each new lift of his hips, and the sound inflamed his control. She was an itch he had to scratch to his satisfaction, a compulsion he couldn't resist. Faster and faster he moved, harder and deeper, and the tension within him shot higher and higher, to an unbearable pitch. He felt himself losing control, his body ripping into a frenzied blur of motion that felt too good, too intense to bear. As his body stiffened and he hung, suspended in a timeless moment of screaming need, he felt her begin her own finish, milking him in repetitive muscular spasms as she thrashed and heaved beneath him, her hips lifting to shove at him time after time. He exploded within her, then, powerful pressures driving him forward and forward again, until he was spent and gasping, every ounce of energy drained.

They lay there for a long, long time before he moved to lie beside her, pulling her over against him with her head in the crook of his shoulder and those marvelous breasts pressed against his side, her hand resting on his chest, palm over his heart.

It occurred to him that this might be a very good time to tell her about himself. But how to begin? "I have something I'd like to tell you," he said, "and I know it's going to upset you a little, but—"

"Let me guess," she said, yawning. "You have five ex-wives stashed around the country."

He chuckled. "Not exactly. But since you brought it up…I was married before. Once. And it only lasted about three years."

"That must be the magic number," she said. Then, while he was still trying to figure out how to lead the conversation around to the place he wanted it to go, she asked, "So what happened? I won't believe you if you tell me you had affairs and rubbed her nose in them."

"Okay, then I won't tell you that." But inside, he was glad that she trusted him. "Sonja and I—just weren't as compatible as we thought we were." He couldn't bring himself to tell her Sonja had married him for his money and he'd been too stupid to catch on until after the fact.

She propped herself on her elbow and looked down at him. "So it just kind of…fell apart?"

"That's about it." *Except that when Sonja fell, she was cushioned by a healthy chunk of my income.* "No big fireworks, no blowouts that required police assistance."

"Lucky you."

That startled him. "You called the cops on dipstick?"

"Once." She lay back, giggling, but quickly sobered. "After we were divorced, he wasn't willing to be civilized. I had been awarded the house, which really got to him, and he periodically came over and ranted and raved. The last time I told him he couldn't come in and he broke the door down. Fortunately I was able to call a friend of mine—oh, you met Jillian, remember?—and when she arrived, he left. Didn't want any witnesses when he murdered me, I guess."

"That's not funny."

"Sorry." She rubbed her palm over his chest and idly played with the flat nipple she discovered, sending sensual messages arrowing straight to his groin. "You know what gets to me the most?" She didn't wait for an answer. "The lying. Later, when he wasn't bothering to hide the women, at least I knew where I stood. But that first time…that first time was devastating. And he lied to me, swore it was never going to happen again. It's the thing I find hardest to forgive."

"Forgive?" It was a weak echo. *Lying. It's the thing I find hardest to forgive.*

"Yes," she was saying. "I'll never want him as a friend, or even an acquaintance, but I've let go of most of the rotten memories. Mostly now I just worry when the boys go with him—hey!"

He'd rolled over onto her, unready for any more intimate discussions, even though it was what he wanted, what he'd planned. Obviously, he was going to have to think this through really carefully before he explained things to her. "I don't want to talk about exes anymore," he said.

She shifted her hips gently beneath him, emphasizing the growing arousal that responded to the feel of her beneath him. "Gee, we'll have to find something to fill the time."

They drove back to Frannie's a few hours later in contented silence. He'd pulled her over to the center seat of the truck to sit beside him, like two teenagers, and she'd chuckled as she put her head on his shoulder.

"Aren't we too old for this?" she asked.

"For what?" He slanted a curious smile her way, keeping most of his attention on the highway.

"Necking in the car, sneaking around behind our families' backs...."

She didn't sound uncomfortable, just amused, and he took the hand he held in his and raised it briefly to his lips. "Right now I don't feel old at all. In fact—" he pulled her hand into his lap "—there's a motel right down the road. We might have time for one more quick round of wild—"

"You're insatiable," she said, exploring his stirring flesh through his pants with purposeful fingers until he pulled her hand away with a groan. She laughed and laid her head against his shoulder. "I think I like 'insatiable.'"

"It's a good thing. I've been walking around in hormone overdrive for weeks. It's going to take a while to get you out of my system." As soon as the words were out of his mouth, he wished he hadn't uttered them. Trying to fix it, he said, "Actually, I think getting you out of my system is impossible. I guess I meant I have to learn to pace myself."

"You don't have to tiptoe around it." Deirdre was still relaxed in his embrace, but there was a distant quality he was pretty sure he wasn't imagining in her voice.

"Tiptoe around what?"

"I don't expect this to last forever." Her words were quiet. He thought they sounded wistful but maybe that was his imagination. "I won't throw fits when you leave. Having this time with you has been the best thing that's happened to me in…well, in years, and I'll always be grateful—''

"I don't want you to be grateful." He realized his hand had tightened on hers, and he made a conscious effort to loosen his grip as he struggled with words that suddenly seemed far too inadequate and confining to explain his feelings. "I don't really know what I expect from what's happening here, but I don't plan on letting you get away. So don't even think about giving me the brush-off, baby."

She was quiet again.

"What?" he finally said. "I hate it when you do that."

"Do what?"

"Think."

"You hate it when I think?" The corners of her lips were curled just the smallest bit, as if she couldn't quite contain her amusement.

He nodded, aware that he sounded fairly idiotic but he was too far in now to get out gracefully. What the hell. Grace had never been his strong suit. "You're thinking something about you and me. And I hate it when I don't know what you're thinking. So give."

"It was nothing earth-shaking. I was only thinking that you can be a real dictator when you want to."

Ah. He didn't particularly like the sound of that. She'd lived with a dictator before, and he sure hoped she wasn't finding any similarities between that ass of an ex of hers and himself. Cautiously he said, "I didn't mean to come off sounding autocratic."

To his astonishment she raised his hand to her lips. "It's okay. I wasn't comparing you to Nelson. You couldn't be less alike."

When they knocked on the door of the Ferrises' home, Jack opened the door. "Hey, come on in," he said, waving with his free hand. He held his infant son securely in the other arm. The child appeared to be sound asleep, tiny features slack and peaceful looking. "Thanks," Deirdre said. "We're a few minutes early."

As Jack closed the door behind them, Ronan took a deep breath of the cool air around them. It was a typically hot, muggy Baltimore summer day, and the respite from the humidity was nice. A television set in the entertainment center in the living room caught his eye, and he turned to Jack as he realized there was a baseball game in progress.

"Is that the O's?"

"Yeah. The game just got started." Jack's eyes were already drifting back to the television. "Come on in and sit down while the women gab."

"Thanks." He turned to Deirdre. "Do you mind?"

"Of course not." She stood on tiptoe and brushed his lips with her own, and his hands came up to her waist, savoring the soft give of her flesh. Suddenly the ball game was much less interesting. Then she slipped away from him and gave him a gentle push. "Go watch the game." She turned to Jack. "Where's Frannie?"

"In the shop," said Jack.

Ronan asked, "What's the score?"

Deirdre was already walking toward the back of the house, and she blew him a smiling kiss. A woman in a million, he reflected. A woman who didn't mind a man watching a little baseball. He took a seat on the edge of the couch, his attention caught when the Sox batter popped up a fly toward right field.

"No runs yet," Jack informed him. "You a fan?"

"Hate to miss a game." *Unless Deirdre wants to play a game just for two. Then there's no contest.*

"Me, too," Jack said. "I'd like to get to one, but since the new stadium was built, decent seats are hard to come by." He grinned, hefting the baby in his arm. "And I haven't exactly had a lot of free time lately."

Erickson was starting tonight for the O's, Ronan noted. Absently he said, "I have season tickets behind the plate.

You're welcome to them sometime.'' As he watched, Rip-ken snagged a line drive and fired an easy toss to first base, closing out the top of the inning. All right.

The Orioles came trotting in toward their dugout—

''Are you kidding?'' his host said.

''About wha—oh.'' Hastily Ronan thought back over his words. Talking about season passes probably wasn't a good idea. And it definitely wouldn't do to tell Jack he had box seats, a half dozen of them. He could tell him another time, after he'd explained everything to Deirdre this evening. ''Not kidding,'' he said. ''I'm a diehard.''

''Well, thanks.'' Jack got up. ''Want a beer?''

''Sure.'' He barely got his arms out before Jack dumped the baby into his lap.

''Back in a minute. Keep an eye on the kidlet for a sec.'' And he vanished into the kitchen.

Ronan awkwardly shifted the baby into a more comfort-able position. Brooks's little face contorted and his body stretched, and Ronan's muscles tensed; he prepared himself for a howl. Then the baby relaxed again, little lips working in a soundless sucking motion.

A bead of sweat dropped from his brow to his knee, just missing the baby's foot. He didn't have a clue what to do with a baby, especially if it started to yell. He wished Jack would hurry back, and halfway through the thought, Jack pushed open the door that led to the kitchen and strode back into the room. He was clutching two cold beers and a bag of pretzels, and he was wearing a broad grin as he plunked a beer down in front of Ronan and retrieved his son.

''Thanks,'' he said.

''Thank you,'' Ronan said. ''I worked up a sweat hold-ing your kid.''

Jack laughed. ''The mere thought of fatherhood make you that nervous?''

Ronan laughed, too. ''You bet.'' He realized Jack

seemed to have accepted his presence a little more gra-ciously this evening, and he was glad. He could see why they were all so protective of Deirdre, but he didn't like being lumped in the Needs Protection From category.

The game had moved into the next inning when he re-alized the time was 7:40. "Hey," he said to Jack. "Weren't the boys supposed to be back by seven?"

Jack glanced at his watch, and his eyebrows rose. "They were."

Ronan rose. "Where would Deirdre be?"

Jack rose, too. "Probably in the kitchen or in Frannie's shop. Come on."

The two women were in the kitchen, and Ronan saw at once that Deirdre was worrying already. Walking around behind her chair, he placed his hands on her shoulders and massaged gently. "Maybe they just got tied up in traffic."

She exhaled slowly. "Maybe. Nelson's been pushing the time limit the past month or so. I didn't say anything be-cause I know he wants to get under my skin. But this is late, even for him." Rising, she wandered into the living room and stood at the front window.

Ronan followed, wishing he could be more reassuring. Anger at her thoughtless ex-husband began to rise, but be-neath it was fear. What if they'd been in an accident? He knew all those thoughts, and more, had to be chasing them-selves around in Deirdre's head, but for now, there was nothing he could do.

Sighing, he flopped back onto the couch as Jack and Frannie came into the room. The bases were loaded and if Palmiero could knock a homer over the fence, the Birds would have a sweet lead.

He couldn't care less.

Six

When Ronan walked over and slipped his arms around her, Deirdre jumped. He realized her attention was so totally focused on the window that she hadn't even heard him approach. "We'll give him a little longer and then try to call him, all right?" he said, rubbing his palms up and down her arms.

She nodded, and he knew she was fighting tears. God, he felt helpless.

They waited until eight, all four of them tensing every time a car turned onto the street. As each one failed to slow and stop, he could feel anxiety pulling at her, stretching her tighter and tighter until he was afraid one more passing vehicle would snap the precarious hold she had on her fear.

At 8:01 he stepped back and turned her away from the window. "I think it's time to make a few phone calls. First, try calling him at home."

She did, letting it ring until a machine picked up and a canned voice instructed her to leave a message. She handed the phone to Ronan without speaking, and he broke the connection.

"Don't call him again," he said. "If he's there and just not answering, he's liable to leave. Where does he live?"

She told him, and he committed the address to memory. "I'll be back in a little while," he said to her.

"Wait! I'm going with you," she cried.

He shook his head. "You're staying here. What if he brings them back? You'll want to be here. If he does have the boys at his house—" he said grimly "—I promise you I'll get them."

She wilted visibly, crossing her arms, anchoring them by holding on to the opposite ones, and he saw that she was going to leave bruises on herself. "You're right."

Gently he worked his fingers beneath hers, lifting them until they were clutching at him rather than her skin. "I'll be back as fast as I possibly can. I promise." He dropped a lingering kiss on her brow, breathing deeply of the sweet, warm woman-scent she exuded before turning to leave.

Jack had been holding the baby. He handed him to Frannie, bent and kissed her quickly. "I'm going with him."

She nodded and he followed Ronan, who was halfway to the truck.

"Hold on," said Jack. "He saw your truck this morning. I just got a new car last week and it was in the garage when he was here. He wouldn't recognize that."

"Good." Ronan wheeled and headed for the garage. "The closer we can get without him knowing we're coming, the better chance we'll have."

Ninety minutes later, they pulled back into Jack's driveway and got out of the car in grim silence. The door opened before they could get two feet, and Deirdre came flying out, her expression alive with hope. "Were they there?"

He'd rather someone pulled his fingernails off than have to tell her they had no luck, but she could see it in his eyes before he spoke. She didn't break down and sob, but one single silent tear welled up and escaped from her lashes, sliding quickly down her cheek and dripping onto her breast. Roughly he pulled her against him, needing comfort as much as he needed to give it. Rationally he knew Lee and Tommy were probably fine, just a little confused about why they hadn't gone home. But his irrational side was a whole lot more active right now, and he seethed with fury at his forced inaction.

He led her into the house, settling her in the rocking chair and squatting so that he was eye level with her. "I think it's time to call the police."

"Oh, God." She put trembling hands to her face. "This isn't a bad dream, it's real. Calling the police will make it real." Her voice died away on the last words, and he pulled her to his chest, giving her what support he could. Silently Jack brought him the cordless phone.

He offered her the phone, but she backed away from it as if it were a snake, shaking her head. "Would you...I can't—"

"I'll call," he said. He stood and punched in the number that Frannie had underlined in the book and waited until it was picked up. The crisp voice at the other end identified the precinct and asked how they could be of help.

"I have a kidnapping to report," he said.

"A kidnapping?" The voice came alert and he imagined the uniformed man sitting up straighter in his chair. "Who was kidnapped, sir?"

"My—" He stopped. "My friend's sons. By their father."

"Oh. We don't get involved in custody problems," the man said. "That's a civil matter."

"So who do I call to report this?"

"I don't have that information. I'll transfer you to a detective, sir," the voice said, and after a moment a new voice came on the line. Ronan repeated his request.

There was silence on the line for a moment after he was

finished. The detective sighed. "We don't, as a rule, get involved in custody disputes. What you need to do is have your friend call her lawyer."

Ronan was silent. He'd been half expecting this, but how was he going to explain to Deirdre that the police weren't going to bring her children back? Finally he said, "Is there any law enforcement agency that would respond to this kind of problem?"

"I doubt it. You have to go through civil court, I think. They won't be open until tomorrow morning." The woman hesitated again. "Look," she said. "I go off duty in half an hour. I live out that way, so how about if I stop by on my way home?"

"We would really appreciate that," he said.

Deirdre's eyes were huge and hopeful when he pressed the button to disconnect.

"We need to call your lawyer," he said, seeing no way to sugarcoat the information. "Law enforcement can't peddle backward fast enough to get away from cases like this."

Frannie came over and put an arm around Deirdre. "I can't believe it. Isn't there anything we can do?"

Ronan shook his head, frustration darkening his face and his mood. "Not without talking to a judge first."

"Are you telling me she isn't going to get them back until she goes to court?"

Deirdre made a sound that was half sob, half moan. "He can't just take them, can he?"

"He already has." Jack drummed his big fingers on the coffee table, his eyes following Ronan as he began to pace around the room. "We need to figure out how to get them back."

Deirdre's face crumpled, wrinkling like carelessly handled tissue paper. For the first time since the ordeal had begun, she began to weep openly. "I can't— They're going to be so— Tommy can't sleep without his alligator." She sobbed harder. "Gumsy keeps him from being afraid in the dark."

Ronan tossed the phone to Jack and went to her. He took her in his arms and sat down on the sofa, rocking her soft body gently and wishing he had her ex-husband in front of him. "Who's her lawyer?" he asked Frannie. "Can you call him?"

She nodded, and he saw that she was gulping, swallowing back her own fears. Quickly she flipped through the phone book and made the call. Ronan only half listened to her end of the conversation. He rubbed Deirdre's back and let her tears soak his shirt, his heart aching for her. He hated feeling so helpless, and his mind raced as he considered and discarded possibilities...most of which would get him thrown in jail.

When Frannie ended the call, she came over and sat down beside them, her hand absently patting Deirdre's knee. "He's going to get something ready tonight," she said. "First thing in the morning he'll file it, and unless he's taken them somewhere else, you'll have them back again in a few days or weeks."

"A few weeks." It was a despairing whisper. Then Deirdre nodded, biting her bottom lip as she tried to compose herself. "Thank you," she said to all of them.

The doorbell rang, and he remembered the cop who'd promised to stop by. As he rose, Jack opened the door and showed a woman in dark pants and a jacket into the room. "This is Detective Sims," he said, introducing each of them.

Detective Sims was about his age, Ronan figured, stocky and athletic with no-nonsense brown hair cropped in a short bob.

Ronan offered his hand. "We spoke on the phone."

The woman nodded, her attention turning to Deirdre. The detective's eyes were soft with compassion as she walked over and sat down facing her. "So your ex took your kids, huh?'' She shook her head. ''We hear this all the time. Wish I could do more for you.''

Then she looked up at Ronan. ''I shouldn't be telling you this, but I have two kids of my own, and I know how I'd feel if this were happening to me.'' She fished a piece of paper out of her pocket. ''This is the number of an old buddy of mine, a former federal agent who retired a few years ago and still likes the occasional challenge. He specializes in finding children who aren't really lost, if you catch my meaning.''

Ronan took the offered paper and scanned the information. ''Does he have office hours or can we call him right now?''

''No office hours. That's his home number.'' She held up one finger when Ronan reached for the phone. ''He doesn't do this for peanuts. Depending on how long it takes to locate 'em, and how difficult it is to get 'em away from the other parent, you might be looking at upwards of ten grand.''

''Ten thousand dollars?'' Deirdre gasped, and the hope that had begun to glow in her eyes dimmed. ''I can't begin to afford that.''

Detective Sims rose. ''It's a hefty chunk of change, no question. But you have to understand—he has all kinds of expenses involved in an undercover job, which is essentially what this would be.'' She took both of Deirdre's hands in hers and squeezed before rising to her feet. ''Good luck getting them back, however you decide to do it.''

After Jack closed the door behind the woman, Deirdre stood and started pacing the room. ''I'll have to sell the farm, I guess.'' She was talking to herself. ''I wonder if he'd be willing to let me pay him in installments?''

Ronan picked up the phone and began to dial the number on the paper. He already knew what he was going to do. He'd deal with the consequences later. ''Don't worry about the money.'' He silenced her with a look when she began

to protest. Then a man's voice answered on the other end
of the line, and he began to negotiate.

Deirdre was still in shock. It was 3:30 in the wee hours
of the morning, and she sat alone in Frannie's kitchen nursing a cup of coffee. Frannie and Jack had finally gone to
bed at her insistence, after midnight came and went. Today
was Monday, and they both would be working.

Edwin Briggs, the man Ronan had hired, was already out
working on finding Lee and Tommy, and Ronan had gone
with him. Briggs had instructed her to wait by the phone
in case Nelson called. And if he did, Briggs had done something to ensure that they would be able to trace the call.
She knew it had to be illegal, not to mention that he probably had had to bribe an employee of the telephone company…and she didn't care one little bit, if it helped find
her sons.

The man Ronan had hired. All three of them—she, Frannie and Jack—had gaped when Ronan had calmly promised
the man on the phone a five-thousand-dollar retainer fee.
That night.

He'd been out the door with his keys in his hand before
she'd even realized the phone conversation had ended.
"Where are you going?" she'd said.

"To get the money." Ronan didn't even slow down.

"But the automatic tellers won't let you withdraw anywhere near that much," Jack had said.

"I know." They'd all followed Ronan to the door and
as he climbed into his truck he'd said, "I have it at home.
I'll be back. If Briggs gets here ahead of me, tell him everything you can."

But Ronan had made it back just as Mr. Briggs arrived.
Briggs was a tall, muscled man with dark hair that shone
with silver highlights. He was calm and quiet, and he'd
gotten her to tell him all kinds of things she knew about

Nelson's habits and hang-outs, things she hadn't even realized she remembered.

"I'm starting now," he informed her. "The warmer the trail, the faster we find 'em."

"There's more than one of you?" Ronan questioned.

Briggs nodded. "I have a few other people working for me as needed. I don't know yet whether or not I'll need to call any of them in."

She'd started to mention money then, but Ronan had cut her off. "Money's no object. Just tell me how much more you need, and you'll have it as soon as the banks open in the morning. The only important thing is that we get the boys back."

That "we" had lightened her spirits for an instant, but the weight of worry replaced it again within seconds. And then there was the little detail of Ronan's money. Bewilderment and confusion were a whirling lump of questions in her mind.

Money was no object. He'd had five thousand dollars just gathering dust in his apartment in her stable. He would get more from the bank in the morning.

Maybe he was simply frugal, saving everything he could. He lived alone, after all. She'd have to pay him back, of course—

The phone rang. She knocked over her coffee cup, thankfully almost empty, and frantically threw napkins on the puddle as she pushed the button to turn the telephone on with trembling fingers. "Hello?"

"We have them." Ronan's voice was filled with jubilation.

"Where are you? Are they all right? How long will it take—"

Ronan laughed. "Whoa, woman. I'm on Briggs's car phone, and we're going over a mountain, so I'd better keep it brief before we lose the connection. The boys are fine. Right now they're asleep in the back seat. Your ex doesn't even know they're gone yet—we took them from a back bedroom of his hunting cabin while he was sleeping in the next room. I'll tell you everything else when we get back.'' His voice deepened. ''Give yourself a kiss for me, and I'll replace it personally in a few hours.''

She could picture the warm glint in his tiger eyes as he spoke, the humorous expression he wore that masked the serious intent in his voice. A warmth shot through her, as tender and sweet as it was arousing. ''I love you, Ronan.''

There was total silence from the other end of the receiver. She could have bitten off her tongue. The words had been a reckless impulse, out before she consciously thought about them. And they would change everything. Miserably she waited, aware that he hadn't responded in any way.

''Deirdre?'' His voice sounded strangely unsure. ''We have to talk when I get home. I'll see you soon, baby.''

She was crying as she hung up, and she wasn't sure if it was happiness that her sons were coming home to her, or fear that she'd just ruined everything with those three stupid little words.

''Who was that?'' Jack came into the kitchen, blinking blearily. He carried Brooks, who looked wide-awake and ready for some fun, in one arm and he took a moment to lay the baby down in a bassinet in the corner.

''That was Ronan. He found them!'' Suddenly she realized what she was saying, and she launched herself at him with a whoop of joy. Jack caught her in midair, hugging her in a ferocious embrace as she pounded his back ecstatically. ''They're safe! He found them,'' she repeated.

''Thank God.'' Jack's voice came from somewhere above her head and she thought it sounded a little shaky. ''Thank God.''

''What's going on in here?'' Frannie stood in the doorway with her hands on her hips. ''First I hear a wild war whoop, then I find my husband flirting. As usual.'' She shook her head fondly, then clasped her hands as if she were praying. "Does this means we have something to celebrate?"

"He found them!" Deirdre charged at her, dragging her into the circle, practically dancing with joy as she clutched Frannie's neck in a stranglehold.

Frannie's eyes filled with tears. "Way to go, Ronan," she said softly. "Now I can cry."

Three hours later the sky had grown light and Monday was waking up, when Briggs's dark blue Suburban glided smoothly into the Ferrises' driveway. Ronan emerged as she came tearing out the front door. He opened the back door of the truck and leaned in, and when he straightened up she saw Lee blinking sleepily in his arms.

As he handed her son to her, their eyes met. And in the instant before he turned away and reached for Tommy, she realized that his gaze was filled with something strong and warm, something that she dared to hope was love.

They drove home with her sons between them.

"Where did Daddy go?" Lee asked. "He said we were staying with him now."

"An' I don' want to," declared Tommy, his lower lip quivering. "He said I'm too big to s'eep wif Gumsy, an' I'm not."

Gumsy…the thought of the big alligator had shattered her earlier. Fury almost choked her now, but she shooed it away, reaching for a calm voice and manner. The last thing the boys needed was to have her flip out. "Daddy's still at the cabin," she said, referring to Nelson's old fishing cabin along the Potomac, where she learned he'd taken them…the cabin she'd forgotten he even owned until Mr. Briggs had jogged her memory. "It was time for you to come home."

She put her arm around Tommy, sitting closest to her, and hugged him tightly. "You can sleep with Gumsy as long as you want to. He's waiting for you on your bed right now." She lowered her voice. "He told me to tell you to hurry home."

Tommy giggled. But Lee wasn't so easily sidetracked. She could almost see the gears turning in that agile little mind which, at five, comprehended the events of the night a bit more accurately than Tommy's did. "I told Daddy he wasn't supposed to take us away overnight, but he said you told him it was okay. You didn't, did you, Mom?"

"No," she said. "Your daddy must have misunderstood me."

"I don't ever want to go away with Daddy again," he said in an aggrieved tone. "He yelled at me when I told him you were going to be mad if he didn't bring us back."

She clenched her teeth together so hard they hurt and counted to ten. "You don't have to do anything with Daddy that you don't want to do, honey," she said.

"Daddy saw Ronan. He said you were going to give us to him since you had Ronan. He said Ronan doesn't like us." Lee shook his head. "An' when I said Ronan liked us, he said, 'Shut up!'"

Both boys' eyes were big and round. *Shut up,* was the worst swear word they knew; one of her rules prohibited the use of the word in her household.

"Daddy was a bad boy," Tommy chirped.

You'd better believe it, she thought. Mulling over Lee's other statements, she worried at the best way to handle the issue of Ronan with her sons. She didn't want them to feel left out or fear that they were being supplanted in her affections, fears that Nelson clearly had tried to encourage.

Then Lee turned to the man driving silently toward her home. "I knew you liked us." He leaned his head against Ronan's side and sighed. "You came and got us."

A muscle worked in Ronan's jaw, and he held Lee close to him for a moment with his free arm. "You got that right, buddy," he said in a husky tone. "I like you."

She leaned her head against the back of the seat, suddenly feeling every minute of the hours of missed sleep dragging at her. How could Nelson have done something so potentially damaging to these two precious babies? They were his *sons,* not something he owned.

And that pretty much said it all, she thought. To Nelson they were property. To her, and to Ronan, they were gifts, to be loved and cherished. When she realized what had just run through her head, she glanced over at the object of her thoughts. Ronan was just pulling into the lane that led to her house, and his attention was on the oncoming traffic. She drank in the straight slope of his nose, the strong jaw covered now with more than his usual day's growth of beard stubble, the high forehead and the single lock of chestnut hair that had fallen over his forehead. Love welled within her, so fierce and deep that she had to take a deep breath to contain herself.

There will be time for us later, she promised herself. Time to share the words, the heart filled with emotions, the act of love that sex had become when she was lying beneath him reveling in her ability to pleasure him as he did her.

After lunch the boys began to drop into a noticeably lower gear, and she made them lie down. "You don't have to sleep," she assured Lee, "just rest on your bed. I know you're too big to take naps anymore."

When she checked on him five minutes later, he was sound asleep, sprawled over the side of the bed with his head hanging down in a terribly uncomfortable looking position. Tommy, across the hall, was curled into a snug ball, as usual, with Gumsy beneath him as a sort of toothy futon.

Smiling to herself, she made her way downstairs with a basket of laundry on her hip. Work awaited, but if she didn't do some laundry soon, the three of them would be reduced to sorting through piles for the cleanest dirty clothes to wear.

As she sprayed grubby little T-shirts with stain remover

before tossing them into the washing machine, she saw Ronan come out of the stable and get into his truck. He was so predictable. Every day, about one o'clock, he went to the post office and did his other chores.

She smiled to herself as she picked up the little bag of chocolate chip cookies she'd made that morning. Perfect timing. As his truck cleared the crest of the hill and disappeared down the lane on the other side, she walked across to the stable, gravel crunching under her feet before giving way to lush green grass again.

It was dim in the stable, with none of the windows open, and she paused to let her eyes adjust to the light. Crossing to the stairs, she heard a telephone ringing and she paused. If it was hers, it might wake the boys. But suddenly the ringing stopped and a machine clicked on, and she realized it was much closer than she'd thought. Ronan must have the ringer at its lowest setting.

Ronan's clear, male voice invited the caller to leave a message after the beep, and a moment later she heard someone begin to speak. It occurred to her that it was rude to eavesdrop, even if it was just a machine, and she began to climb the stairs, intent on leaving the cookies and getting back to her work.

"Hey, Ronan! Good news! Pick up the phone." The caller didn't identify himself. "Dammit, Ronan, I know you're sitting there thinking, 'Oh, hell, it's my lousy agent again.' But I have to talk to you! I'm sorry if you're in the middle of a critical scene, but this is big!"

A pause, as the man waited for Ronan to pick up. She froze, halfway up the steps, unable to pinpoint the sudden dread that immobilized her. The moment lasted forever as she balanced on a knife edge, unable to name the fear but knowing that something was about to change in her life if she didn't get away from that impatient voice...but she couldn't move.

Then the choice was taken from her.

"All right, you win. Just listen. And if you're really not home, call me back pronto! We just got an offer from— are you sitting down?—StarVision Pictures. They want to make a movie version of *Among the Cold at Heart*! The original offer is for five, but given the box office appeal your name will give it, I think we should negotiate for more.... Call me as soon as you get in, and we'll talk about the particulars. Ciao, you gold mine, you."

The machine clicked off as the caller hung up at the other end, but the words were still echoing in her ears. *StarVision Pictures...movie version...gold mine....*

She couldn't get her lungs to work, couldn't get enough air and she sat down heavily on the step. *Among the Cold at Heart* had been a bestselling novel last year. She read all the books that made the *New York Times* list, and that book had been a particular favorite. She'd read several earlier works by the author, R. J. Sullivan, Ronan. Her Ronan Sullivan.

No, not hers. Her Ronan was a journalist.

But contradictions, nasty little memories, kept surfacing. He'd been strangely uncomfortable any time she'd mentioned his work, but she'd taken it as a sign that he wasn't having a lot of luck selling. Hah! The money he'd been so blasé about shelling out—

Oh, God, the money. She didn't even know how much he'd eventually paid Mr. Briggs, the child finder, but she knew it was more than she could easily raise. And to Ronan, it must have been peanuts. No, peanut shells. The agent's words hammered in her head again. The original offer was for five. Five million? Even as she shrank from it, she knew it had to be so.

Ronan, the man who'd made love to her, the man who had invaded her heart the first day he'd hunkered down in the dirt to talk to her sons, was R. J. Sullivan, national bestselling author of five—or was it six?—suspense novels.

He made more money in one phone call than she would in her entire life.

Waves of betrayal battered her. The bag of cookies dropped from her hand and lay, a broken pile of pieces at her feet. He'd lied to her. From the very first day they'd met again, he'd lied to her.

He'd lied about his job.

He'd surely lied about needing a place to live.

And his lovemaking, all the wild and passionate, tender and caring moments he'd shared with her…all those had been a lie, too. They must be. She wasn't the kind of woman a celebrity would seek out.

Except for a little convenient sex.

She stuffed her hand into her mouth as a sudden, loud sob broke free. But nothing could contain the ache in her heart that grew and widened and swelled until she was weeping steadily: harsh, gasping breaths that left her throat raw; hot, boiling tears that set her eyes on fire. She pressed the heels of her palms against them, but the tears squeezed out, anyway.

She crawled down the steps, one painful inch at a time, and made her way from the stable, her whole body convulsed. She'd trusted him. Finally, she'd thought, after paying for the mistake of her marriage for so many years, she'd finally found someone to love. To love her.

And she'd been stupid enough to be taken in by a liar for the second time.

The boys woke up two hours later. From the kitchen she heard them on the portable monitor. The first stretch and rustle was Lee. He climbed off his bed and she heard little footsteps making a beeline for his brother's room.

Quickly she grabbed the bowl of peas she'd picked up at the local market, and headed for the back porch, setting her sunglasses on her nose to cover her swollen eyes. She felt dull, disoriented. If only she could simply go to bed and not be bothered by the world for a few hundred years.

Maybe then, the exposed nerves of her feelings would be deadened enough for her to pretend normalcy.

As she settled in the rocking chair, Murphy heaved his bulk out from beneath the lilac bush and came up the steps to lie at her feet. Oh, how she envied him! If only she could just lie down without a care in the world.

But she couldn't just go to bed. She had two little boys to take care of. Two little boys who'd had a very traumatic experience yesterday, two little boys who needed her. The bowl of peas awaited, but she just sat there, staring into nothing.

Nothing. That's what her future held.

"Hey, Mom, can we have a snack?"

"There are strawberries in the refrigerator."

"Huh?"

"There are strawberries in the refrigerator."

Lee appeared at the back door, Tommy and Gumsy trailing behind. "Mom, you sound funny. What'd you say?"

She repeated herself again, and the boys paraded back into the kitchen. Lee was right. She did sound funny. She was hoarse, courtesy of two hours of crying. Hoarse to the point of barely being able to make a sound.

She picked up a pea and shelled it, tossing the pod into a paper bag on the floor. Automatically she repeated the motion, trying to block out all thought except ones that pertained to the vegetables in front of her.

Her sons came back outside with the strawberries and sat on the steps.

Murphy leaped to his feel with a bark of greeting, giving her a second's notice before Ronan came around the corner of the house.

She surged out of the rocker, the pea bowl dropping to the floor. Peas rolled across the porch, but she didn't even notice. She hadn't heard him return and she wasn't ready for this. Her stomach jolted; panic stole her breath. She couldn't face him yet.

"Tell Ronan I'm sick," she said to the boys as she yanked open the door and dashed into the house.

She went straight to her bedroom, where she sat on the edge of her bed with her hands clasped in her lap to keep them from shaking. Her insides felt jittery, as if she would throw up if she thought much about it, so she concentrated on taking deep breaths. Deep, calming breaths.

She absolutely could not deal with seeing him right now. Eventually, she knew, she would have to. And "eventually" probably meant tomorrow, if she knew Ronan.

You *don't* know him, a little voice in her head reminded her with brutal frankness. *He deliberately lied to you, told you he was something he wasn't. And you fell for it. Hard.*

The boys' footsteps pounded up the stairs and headed down the hall toward her room. What was she going to tell them about Ronan? How were they going to feel when he left?

Deep, calming breaths.

"She's in here," said Tommy as he appeared in the doorway. He was pointing triumphantly at her, and her heart tore completely in half, raggedly ripped right down the middle, when Ronan followed him into the room.

Seven

"Thanks, guys," Ronan said to the kids, forcing a note of normalcy into his voice, although he felt anything but normal right now. "You can go back outside now."

Lee looked from Ronan to his mother, clearly uncertain. The child was picking up the high-voltage emotion running around the room, Ronan figured, and he knew something didn't feel right. "What are you gonna do?" Lee said in response.

"I need to talk to your mom for a few minutes, and then I'll take you down to the creek if it's okay with her."

"All right!" It was Lee's favorite expression of delight; Ronan had heard it dozens of times in the weeks he'd lived here. As he had hoped, the promise of a dip in the creek was enough to divert Lee's attention from the adults. "C'mon, Tommy."

Both boys trotted off, sufficiently bribed, and in a minute he heard them heading down the stairs, sounding more like a troop of elephants than two little kids.

He looked across the room at Deirdre, sitting on the edge of her bed, and he realized they might as well be miles apart. Her face was white, and even through the sunglasses she still wore, he could tell she'd been crying. Hell! Of all the lousy timing—he'd been going to tell her yesterday, and the opportunity simply hadn't arisen. He'd been going to tell her today....

"You heard, didn't you? You heard the message." His chest felt like somebody had forced him to swallow rocks.

She nodded, staring at him as if he might attack her any second.

"Dammit!" He slammed his fist against the solid wooden door frame so hard the thunk shook the wall.

She jumped, a harsh gasp forcing its way past her swollen vocal cords.

"I was going to tell you," he said, flexing his fingers to check for broken bones.

She turned her head away, staring out the window, swallowing visibly.

"Baby, talk to me." He knew he was pleading but he didn't care. How the hell could he fix it when he didn't know what was broken?

"I don't have anything to say." Her voice was a scratchy whisper, and still she didn't look at him.

"Are you feeling bad? Your voice sounds terrible." Maybe she was so upset because she was sick. When he didn't feel good, little things got blown all out of proportion—

"No." She turned her head then and looked at him, and the total lack of life in her eyes was a knife in his heart. "I was crying earlier. Someone I cared for died."

He winced, knowing full well what she meant. "Deirdre, let me explain. It's just not as simple—"

"Get out!" She might not have volume but there was enough vehemence in her poor ruined voice to shake him right out of his shoes. "You lied to me." Tears began to roll out from under the sunglasses. "I trusted you, and you lied to me."

"Baby." He was across the room in two strides, reaching for her. She fought him, silently fighting against the bands of strength he wrapped around her, twisting and heaving until the sunglasses clattered to the floor, sobs rushing in and out as she tried to get away. But he wasn't about to let her go, and finally she stopped struggling. He'd pulled her into his lap in his efforts to keep her from landing a solid blow; he tucked her head under his chin and rocked her as he had last night when the thought of Tommy without his alligator had broken her determined effort at control.

She would forgive him. She had to. "I didn't lie to you," he started. "Well," he amended, "I did, but not to you, specifically. When people learn who I am, they tend to want me to behave like they think a celebrity should. Although I'm damned if I know how. In the past couple of years, I've tried not to attract the attention of the public. Even so, it had gotten so there was always somebody at my condo wanting autographs, introductions…you can't imagine what it's like. Writers trying to get published even bring me their manuscripts and expect that I'll have the time to read them and offer my opinions."

He stopped to gauge the effect of his words, but she wasn't moving. She wasn't giving off any signals, any clues to what she was thinking. That was a good sign. She was thinking over his words, seeing that this really wasn't anything to fight about. "Several years ago I started getting some pretty kooky mail from a fan. The woman started showing up at my apartment, following me when I shopped or took a walk. One day I found her in my apartment, in my bed! She was arrested, finally, but I don't want to go through something like that again. When I decided to move out of Baltimore, I—"

"You expect me to believe you chose to move out of a condo—complete with doorman and maid service, no doubt—to live *over my stable?*'' She shoved at his chest, catching him by surprise, stunning him into speechlessness as he gaped at this madwoman who had taken the place of his quiet, gentle Deirdre with the hidden flame that only he could fan into a wild, hungry blaze.

She leaped away from him and whirled, poking herself in the chest for emphasis as she hurled the words at him. ''I wasn't just, 'the public,' Ronan.'' She paused, and a deep shadow passed over her face. ''But I guess I was to you. Just somebody to entertain you until you got tired of the simple life and went back to where you belong.''

''Which is where?'' He'd recovered the power of speech. And with it came a welcome anger, fury so great he was actually shaking. She had taken every word he'd said and twisted it into some alternate reality, and she'd closed her mind to anything he might say to challenge it.

''Not here, that's for sure!''

''You're not going to give me a chance, are you? Just because you had one lousy experience with a man doesn't mean the next one will be the same. You told me you loved me last night. Was it true?''

She pressed a hand to her mouth, backing away until she banged into the wall beside the door. But she didn't answer him.

''You accused me of lying,'' he said, knowing he was holding himself in check by the slimmest of threads. ''But you're just as bad.'' His eyes narrowed as he stalked her, moving across the room to look into her eyes, those beautiful emerald eyes in which he once thought he saw his future. The frozen tundra he saw now cut to the bone; he turned grief into self-protective rage, wanting—needing—her to see how little her rejection mattered to him. He'd been down this road once before with a woman he'd thought he loved; no way was he going to let Deirdre think she'd gotten to him, that she mattered.

''You wanted sex, and I happened to be holding the

lucky number. Women.'' He spat out the word with all the contempt he could dredge up, ignoring the horrified sound that shoved its way out of her strained throat. ''You want men for sex, for money, for power, and you dress up that hunger as 'love.'''

He walked through the door and down the hall, determined never to look back, in case she thought she'd hurt him. ''Don't snoop around the stable anymore. If you want to look inside the apartment, just ask. *Landlady*.''

When was he leaving?

It had been three weeks since the day Ronan had destroyed her dreams. Long, hellish weeks in which she'd had to force herself to perform even simple tasks. Caring for the boys took all her energy. At night she fell into bed, so exhausted that she didn't even dream. Which she considered a blessing. Sweet oblivion. Her only regret was that morning came.

They hadn't spoken since he'd stormed out of her bedroom. The boys had acted as unwitting messenger service on the few occasions there'd been a need for contact.

''Mom, Ronan says he'll take us up in the meadow to fly the kite. Okay?''

''Mom, Ronan said to tell you he's going to be away for four days.'' Where had he gone?

''Mom, Ronan took Murphy for his walk.''

''Mommy, Ronan told me to give you this.'' ''This,'' was an envelope containing the month's rent they'd agreed upon. She'd squashed the tiny flare of happiness that he would be here for at least another month.

Her days were quiet. She rarely left the farm except for necessary shopping, church and things like doctor's and dentist's appointments for the boys.

Lee and Tommy hadn't gone with Nelson on Sundays since he'd taken them to the hunting cabin. Her lawyer had filed a motion asking that he be denied visits on the grounds that he wasn't reliable and that there was the potential for abuse. The judge had decreed that any future visits would be at her discretion, that Nelson wasn't to contact her except through their lawyers and that he could not speak to the boys unless she so chose.

A week and a half had passed peacefully afterward; Lee had finally realized in the middle of the following week that they hadn't gone with Daddy on Sunday. The patent relief both her sons displayed made her sure she was doing the right thing, as she carefully explained that if and when they wanted to see Daddy, they could tell her and she would arrange it.

"Nuh-uh," said Tommy, shaking his short-cropped black head vigorously. "Daddy doesn't like Gumsy."

Lee was more astute. "If we go with Dad, he might take us away again, right?"

"It's a possibility," she'd been forced to admit. "But your daddy loves you, honey. He thought he was doing the right thing, even if we know he wasn't."

"Well, I don't care," Lee said, his lower lip puckering. "He scared me, Mom. So I don't ever wanna go with him without you."

Her little warrior. Lee rarely cried; that the suggestion of a parental visit with his father should have him struggling with tears told her far more than words ever could have.

"But I'd go with Ronan."

Five little words, uttered by a child too young to know the fresh devastation they left in their wake.

She worked, because there was nothing else, and the children didn't require her attention every minute. Even through a bout of the flu she hadn't completely shaken, she worked. She finished the New York order and started one from an Ohio toy shop. Jillian also had given her a small order. Normally, she didn't do quantities less than half a dozen, but this was Jill. She intended to use the little ghost and witch as a Halloween display in her children's toy store in Downingtown Plaza, a store where Deirdre invariably spent far too much money any time she went near the place.

Christmas was still half a year away, but toy stores all over the nation were gearing up for the big spending season. She was beginning to get calls from people she'd never heard of, people to whom one of her satisfied customers had shown her creations, people who wanted her work in their stores. She should have been thrilled. Extra income meant that she'd have a cushion when things were slow, a cushion that didn't exist at this point.

But she couldn't summon the energy to care.

She was her own worst enemy. Every time she turned around, she was thinking of Ronan.

One of her thoughts was practical, necessary. She had to pay him back for the money with which he'd hired the man to find the boys. No way was she going to let him assume that cost. They were her children, and it was her responsibility. And she'd pay him back somehow if it took every extra dime she ever made.

Other thoughts weren't so practical. She could barely stand to sit on the porch anymore…memories of that first shattering night he'd touched her reduced her to tears. Never mind that the evening had ended so badly. All she could recall now was driving need, frantic possession, lingering tenderness.

But you might have another reminder one of these days.

With determined concentration, she banished the thought and brought the pressure foot on her sewing machine down. She carefully guided the dark purple velvet that was evolving into a cape for a princess, her foot on the pedal sure and steady as she governed the needle's speed.

It wasn't a new sewing machine. It had been a high-school graduation gift from her parents, back in the days when she'd still had stars in her eyes and the world awaiting her. Her throat grew tight as she realized that life had extinguished the stars, and the future was just one more thing to be gotten through.

Absently she patted the sewing machine again, craving the innocence that came with the memories of receiving it. It had been a surprise, a gift that had thrilled her as no silver or gold ever could. She would never part with it, but sometimes she longed to walk into a shop and purchase a new one. There were machines out there today that could practically sew by themselves. All a seamstress had to do was program the internal computer correctly, an incredible time-saving device ensuring accuracy. She'd looked at them for several years, even asked for one for birthday and Christmas rolled together, but Nelson hadn't seen the need to indulge her "little hobby." And now...now she barely had enough money to pay the bills at the end of the month and set aside a tiny bit toward the boys' educations. It would be a few more years before she could think about a new one.

It might be more than a few more years if what you suspect is true.

With a weary sigh she laid her head on the edge of the cabinet that housed her sewing machine. There was no use in ignoring her fears; they intruded into everything she did.

She hadn't had her period since that first time with Ronan. Six, almost seven weeks ago. In the bathroom cupboard, a home pregnancy test lurked, staring her in the eye every time she reached for her toothpaste. Twice this week she'd gone so far as to take it from the shelf and read the directions.

And twice she'd put it back again. Maybe her period was just late because she'd been so upset recently, out of her routine. And maybe the unrelenting nausea she'd been fighting really was just a flu bug hanging on. She'd lost eight pounds, which thrilled her, but she had no appetite. She noticed everything she ate tasted like chalk—when she could force herself to eat it at all. Sleep came sporadically, and even when it did, the dreams came with it, and she'd wake with the pillow soaked with tears, hoping she hadn't awakened the boys by crying aloud.

She was getting a tremendous amount of sewing done, though, with the frequent midnight-to-dawn work sessions. And Murphy was in seventh heaven, being invited into the house almost every night rather than sleeping in his kennel.

But she couldn't put it off any longer. Her conscience wouldn't let her. If she was pregnant, she needed to go to a doctor, take vitamins, stop drinking coffee. If she was pregnant, then the baby deserved the same careful nurturing her other pregnancies had received.

The next morning she tiptoed into the bathroom before the boys were up. Even the sun was just waking. She hadn't gone to bed until 2:00 a.m., and her eyes were gritty and her senses dull.

Her fingers trembled as she took down the package, fumbling with the wrapping so badly that she nearly dropped it. Quickly she followed the directions, eyes on her watch until time was up. She looked at the little stick. And her heart stopped.

No! Oh, God, please. No.

What was she going to do?

Adrenaline was pouring through her system as if she'd run a fifty-yard sprint. She realized she was gulping air like water, and she forced herself to breathe slowly, as a wave of dizziness eddied through her and the edges of her vision grew dark. Her stomach rolled, and she realized she was going to throw up.

Afterward, she wiped her face with a damp cloth. The pregnancy test kit still lay on the counter, and she shuddered. Dropping the whole awful thing into the trash can, she stumbled back to bed.

She couldn't pretend anymore. She couldn't make up stupid excuses for her body's failure to do its normal things, couldn't pretend she had the flu dead smack in the middle of the summer.

She was going to have Ronan's baby.

At the thought of telling him she was pregnant, she moaned aloud. How could she bring a child into the world, knowing that its father hated its mother? And its mother...well, she didn't hate him. She just hurt.

But even as the thoughts crossed her mind, she knew that bearing this child wasn't a choice. Not for her. Not ever. She would love this baby, no matter what mistakes she might have made in her brief relationship with the child's father. Being pregnant again was definitely not the best news she'd ever had, especially if she got as sick as she had both other times in the first trimester, but she refused to allow it to become the worst. A life was precious. A child was precious, a gift parents should cherish.

When she remembered the last time she'd thought that, tears came to her eyes again. It had been the night the boys were kidnapped—a term she hated, but there was no pretty way to say it. Ronan had shown her with his actions since he'd met her sons that they enchanted him, and that night she'd sensed his fear as surely as she knew her own.

Ronan might not be happy when he found out he was a father, but at least she knew their child would never be neglected, never be unloved.

Ronan looked at the calendar again. He should have had the first six chapters finished by now. Hell, he should have had it finished last week. He was due to start the script for *Among the Cold at Heart* in six months. At the rate he was going, he'd still be in chapter five.

Work was—for the first time since he'd started writing—work. He felt like he was slogging through knee-deep mud in every scene. Every sentence, every word, bore the blood he'd sweated trying to produce them.

It was just no fun. Not even writing a script for a movie

made from one of his books, which should have been a thrill, appealed to him.

It was her fault. He tried to dredge up the rage that had carried him through the first week, but it had long since drained away, leaving him hollow, emptied of venom and, though it galled him to admit it, lonely and sad.

He'd had a good reason for what he did, dammit. Like he'd tried to explain, he hadn't lied to her on purpose. It had been a generic, cover-all-the-bases reflex at first, and he simply hadn't figured out how to fix it.

And then it blew up in his face.

How come she hadn't even given him the benefit of the doubt? How come she'd condemned him without even a trial? She was a witch, and he was glad he didn't have to see her anymore.

And pigs flew.

So what? So what if you miss her so damn bad you've nearly gone over there and shaken her until she listened to you.

His body hadn't forgotten her; it reminded him of her on a regular basis. Even when he'd been six thousand miles away, meeting starlets and sweethearts in Hollywood while his agent negotiated the contract for the screenplay, his body's reaction had been markedly unenthusiastic…until night came and Deirdre slipped into his dreams.

But that didn't matter. She didn't want him. And he didn't want her. And he would prove it. He'd only paid that additional month's rent to show her she couldn't chase him away. Although she hadn't exactly tried. He'd laid eyes on her approximately once a day since they'd ended it, and that was only from a distance when she was going to and from her Bronco. She was never on the porch anymore when he went around to get Murphy. She was rarely even close by in the kitchen. Most of the time the boys had to run elsewhere in the house to give her messages.

Her workroom. He knew she was spending half the night

working in there. He knew because midnight walks had begun to appeal to him recently. He'd just happened to notice her silhouette against the light as she moved around the room—

He wasn't going to let her get to him, dammit!

Then he gave a huge sigh. Who was he kidding with his stupid denials? Not himself. And there sure as hell wasn't anybody else around to kid. Since the day he'd found that bag of shattered cookies on his steps, his life had been shattered, too.

He'd thought she was different from Sonja. And she had been. She hadn't cared about his money, hadn't wheedled or cajoled him into buying her expensive trinkets. A memory of their day at the harbor forced itself into her head. In fact, she'd been determined not to let him spoil her or her sons.

When she'd told him she loved him, he was just a journalist to her. Okay, so she hadn't been after his money. Maybe she'd had some other motive. He knew firsthand how women could dress up any motive as love. Maybe she really believed she loved him. But she hadn't, not really. She couldn't.

If it hadn't been just the sex, she never would have cut him out of her life over something as stupid as that misunderstanding. Not if she'd really loved him.

High-pitched giggling, followed by the sound of little footsteps on the stairs, alerted him that Oops and I'm Sorry, as he'd privately and affectionately begun to think of Tommy and Lee, were hunting him. With a sense of relief, he hit Save and turned off his PC. Maybe tomorrow would be better.

He met them at the top of the stairs, hurling one over each shoulder and running down the steps as fast as he could, provoking wild screams punctuated with more giggles. Outside the stable, he set them on their feet, Lee first, and then smaller Tommy. "Hey, guys, are you going swimming with me today?"

Two pairs of little eyes lit up. "Yeah!" Two pairs of little legs wheeled to dash off toward the house for towels. They never bothered with suits since the group was all guys—an important distinction in Lee's eyes now that he was an old man of five—then the little rascal stopped and rushed back.

"Almost forgot. Mom wants to talk to you. She said could you come over after supper?"

Ronan nodded as Lee trotted away, but his voice had temporarily deserted him. What could she want?

Maybe she wanted to apologize. He was willing to forget the whole miserable quarrel if she was.

But more likely, he thought darkly, she wanted to tell him to quit playing with her kids. Or that his monthly lease wasn't going to be renewed in September.

From that point on, the afternoon stretched and lengthened until he was sure somebody was messing with his watch. After the swim they returned to the house, and he got Murphy for their daily walk.

He ate a solitary meal of canned ravioli, while the boys went into the house for their mother's home-cooked dinner, and retrieved his e-mail, and at last it was 7:00. Surely supper could be considered "over" at this time. At least, for anybody with little kids.

Trying not to hurry, he took his time crossing the yard and walking around to the back of the house. The dog whined ecstatically when he saw him, and he made himself take a moment to stop and scratch Murphy's belly before walking up the steps and knocking on the screen door.

"Come on in." Her voice sounded normal enough. "But let the dog stay outside for now, please."

He pulled open the screen door and stepped into the comfortable world she had created in her kitchen. Familiar smells assailed his nostrils: cinnamon, something floral from the vase on the table, various mild herby odors wafting down from the bundles suspended just above his head. She was standing at the sink with her back to him, and as he looked at her, he realized his palms were sweating. Surreptitiously, he wiped them on his pants.

The first thing he noticed was that she'd lost weight. Enough weight that the rounded hips he'd loved were slender and svelte—no, actually skinny—beneath her jeans. It was fashionable, and he knew women did a lot of strange things to achieve this kind of goal but he preferred her the way she had been before.

Then she turned around, and he was shocked anew. Unpleasantly so. Her face was gaunt. His writer's mind flipped through, "emaciated," "thin" and "hollow-cheeked," but ultimately settled on the first word that had sprung to mind. Her cheeks were hollow, in keeping with the fragile appearance of the rest of her, but the rest of her face looked drawn and tired. As far as he could see she wore no makeup, not even to cover the dark circles beneath her eyes, and her lips were pale and dry. She looked like absolute, living hell.

It was all he could do not to take her in his arms and make her rest for about a hundred days.

"Hello," she said quietly. "Would you prefer to sit here or in the living room?"

"This is fine," he said. "Where are the boys?"

The merest trace of a smile tugged at her lips briefly. "In Tommy's room, playing with the elaborate Lego village they've been building all week. At least, I hope that's what they're doing."

He nodded, but found that smiling was out of the question. "Are you sick?" He blurted out the question without thinking, then realized he'd opened with practically the same words the last time they'd spoken.

She shook her head, eyes on the tablecloth, where her fingers were pleating and smoothing and repleating a section of the fabric, over and over and over. "Just tired. I've been working a lot."

"You look like you're more than tired." He couldn't hide his concern. When he saw the quick surge of alarm that flared in her eyes before she controlled her expression, he was more than concerned; he was scared.

"I'll be fine." She waved her hand, dismissing the topic, and though he wanted to demand she tell him what was really wrong with her, her distant courtesy fell like an invisible barrier between them. "I wanted to talk to you about the money you spent last month when—the day—"

"I know when." His voice was harsh; he was so damn disappointed he stood and turned away, staring down into the dormant fireplace. "That's why you asked me to come over here?"

"Yes." It was a mere thread of sound. "I want to set up a schedule to repay your loan. With interest, of course."

"That wasn't a loan," he said through his teeth. "That was a gift."

"I can't accept it. I want to repay the money."

"No."

"I won't accept a gift of that magnitude. I appreciate it—" Her voice stumbled. "You know how much it meant to me."

"Then why won't you forget about it? It's not like I'll miss it." Her eyelids flinched, and he realized that hadn't been the most intelligent thing he could have said. "Look." He tried again. "Those little guys mean a lot to me, too. I was glad I could help. Please stop worrying about paying me back." God, she was stubborn. He hadn't really believed his own conclusions until now, had thought that deep down, she could be swayed by the thought of his wealth. He couldn't have been more wrong.

And she was still shaking her head. "Ronan, I won't take money from you. I saw it as a loan then, and I see it the

same way now. I appreciate everything you did that day—''
She stopped abruptly.

The sound of his name on her lips actually hurt, he discovered. Why did this woman have such power over him?
He'd sworn he'd never be manipulated by a woman again,
and yet here he was, sick with worry—and longing, too—
over this one. "I'm glad you appreciated everything I did,"
he said, to keep her from seeing that she was getting to
him. "Although you don't have to say it. I could tell from
the way you let me appreciate you that you liked it."

She was silent, and he turned, anger a hard knot in his
chest. "You liked it a lot, if my memory is correct."

"Ronan, please…" There was anguish in her voice. "I
don't want it to be like this. Not now."

"Not now?" he sneered, rage and pain making him want
to hurt her as much as she was hurting him. "Then when?
How long are you going to pretend you didn't like it? Why
don't we just consider the loan paid off for a little 'afternoon delight'?"

She stood so abruptly her chair overbalanced and went
crashing to the floor behind her. There were tears in her
eyes. "I won't listen to this." She swallowed hard. "I *will*
repay you, somehow, whether or not you—" Suddenly her
eyes widened and she turned. Without another word, she
rushed from the room.

Astonished, still enraged, he started down the hall after
her but stopped as the door of the downstairs bathroom
slammed shut in his face. And as he stood there, seething,
an unmistakable sound assaulted his ears. Deirdre was losing her dinner, retching repeatedly, over and over again
until there couldn't possibly be anything left to come up.

"Deirdre?"

Silence.

"Dee! Answer me!"

She didn't, though the toilet flushed.

"I'm coming in," he warned her.

"No." He could water running in the sink. "I'll be out in a minute."

"I'm timing you." He leaned one shoulder against the wall, prepared to stay there until she came out. She was sicker than she wanted to let on, and a sense of shame swept over him as his callous words of moments ago rang in his ears.

After another few seconds the door opened and she emerged. She looked even worse, if that was possible, than she had before, and as he moved forward he said, "You're going to bed. And you're staying there until this flu or whatever it is, goes away. I'll take care of the boys."

"No!" She pushed at his chest, but it was a feeble imitation of the fury with which she'd fought him the day she found out who he was, and he gathered her in his arms and carried her up the stairs. "I can't go to bed. I have too much—"

"Shut up," he said through his teeth. How much weight had she lost? She felt like a feather in his arms and she hadn't been heavy before. "Just shut up or I swear to God I'll put a gag in your mouth."

As he set her on her bed, her sons appeared, eyes wide and round.

"You said 'shut up!'" Lee informed him. In case he didn't know.

"We're not allowed to say that," Tommy said.

"I'm not allowed to say it, either." He stripped the sheets down and laid her on the mattress.

"What's wrong with Mommy?"

"She's not feeling so good," he said. "But when she gets better, she'll probably wash my mouth out with soap."

Both boys giggled, but Lee's little face sobered quickly. "Mom doesn't feel good all the time. Are you gonna take her to the doctor?"

"That's a good idea. I just might." He made an effort to smile at them, aware that they would get alarmed if they thought he was. "I promise I'll take good care of her. Would you guys do something for me?"

They both nodded eagerly.

"Go downstairs and get a big glass of ice water for Mom. Then get a washcloth and make it wet and bring it to me. Bring a towel, too," he added.

"Okay."

As they headed down the stairs, he turned his attention back to Deirdre. She hadn't even argued while he was issuing directions, and that was possibly the scariest sign of all that something was seriously wrong. He set his hands at her waist and started to unfasten her jeans.

Her hands came up over his and she shook her head. "No."

"I'm only going to make you more comfortable."

"No."

"Yes." He yanked open the snap and tugged down her zipper, then stripped the jeans away. As his hands went to the buttons of the sleeveless blouse she wore, he tried to hold on to his composure, not to let her see how shaken he was. He'd never seen anybody lose this much weight in…a month? She made a single whimpering sound when he unfastened her bra, slipping it off with the blouse. Looking around, he saw a short sleep shirt hanging beside a robe on hooks on the back of the door. He snagged it and sat on the edge of the mattress to tug it over her head, and as she pulled her arms through the sleeves, the garment caught around her shoulders, hanging above her naked breasts as if to frame them. He couldn't help looking, couldn't have looked away if a husband with a shotgun had come into the room. In contrast to the rest of her too-slender frame, her breasts seemed even lusher and fuller than before; they rose from her slender torso like perfectly ripe melons, just waiting to be plucked.

A sudden surge of desire rushed through him, making him so hard so fast he almost groaned aloud. Another time, she wouldn't have known what was happening until he was inside her, dragging her legs up around him— He couldn't stand, or she'd know what he'd been thinking. He reached out and put a hand to her forehead as she tugged the shirt down and lay back on the pillow.

She rolled her head away. "Stop it."

"Petulance doesn't become you." But he was relieved; she didn't seem abnormally hot. Still, she obviously wasn't well. He put one hand down on the bed on each side of her shoulders, leaning over her. "I'm calling a doctor."

"I'm not sick." Her eyes had been closed, but she opened them enough to glare at him. "I just need some rest."

"Uh-huh. I'm calling a doctor. Now you can tell me which one or I'll open the phone book and dial the first number I see."

She was silent, staring up at him with huge eyes. She looked so stricken that he felt pity stir in his chest.

"Baby," he said, "We can sort out our problems later. You can hit me over the head for strong-arming you and never speak to me again, if that's what you want. But please let me call a doctor."

Her green eyes were deep pools of doubt. Finally her frowning brows relaxed fractionally. So did he. She was going to let him call the doctor.

"I don't need a doctor," she said. "I'm pregnant."

Eight

I'm pregnant I'm pregnant I'm pregnant… The words ricocheted around the room like carelessly fired bullets, bouncing from surface to surface with the incessant energy of well-fed fleas. Deirdre closed her eyes, unwilling to let Ronan see the tears that fought to fall free.

He hadn't shown any shock, any emotion, not even the flicker of an eyelash, at her announcement. Now he turned away, picking up the clothing he'd discarded as he'd undressed her, hanging her things on the hook behind the door.

Finally there was nothing left to hang. But still he stood with his back to her. Clearly too dismayed to face her, she thought.

"What did the doctor say about your weight loss?"

Now it was her turn to be silent for a moment. "I haven't been to the doctor."

"What?" He spun back to her, anger etched on his features. "You've been this sick and you haven't been to a doctor?"

"I have an appointment scheduled for the end of next week," she said defensively.

"If you haven't seen a doctor, how do you know you're pregnant?"

She glared at him. "I've done this twice before, remember?" She looked away toward the window so he wouldn't see the tears that rose again. He sounded as if he hoped she was mistaken.

"You still need to see a doctor right away," he said. "I don't have a lot of experience with pregnant women, but I know this isn't normal."

"Morning sickness is quite common. It usually passes after the first three months or so. And I felt just like this with both of the boys."

"Yes, but you haven't seen a doctor yet. You could be wrong—"

"I took one of those do it yourself tests," she said fiercely. "I'm not wrong."

"All right," he said. "Just checking." There was a silence. "You still need to go to a doctor. Is there one you want me to call?"

"I don't—"

Ronan picked up the phone that sat in a cradle by her bed and started punching in numbers.

"What are you doing?" she asked in alarm.

"Calling information." His voice was hard and clipped. "You're going to the first obstetrician I can get hold of."

"Wait!" she said.

He paused, and the coolness in his eyes when he looked at her made her want to shiver.

"I use Dr. Payne. He delivered both boys." Reluctantly she gave him the number.

He pushed the buttons, but when she reached for the

phone, he held it out of reach. "Nope. I'm doing the talking."

Annoyed, she huffed out a breath. He was acting like she'd committed a crime or something. Folding her arms, she rolled her eyes to the ceiling, letting him know what she thought of these caveman tactics as he spoke to the receptionist.

"She has an appointment next week," he said into the phone, "but she's been terribly ill and I need to speak to the doctor.... Yes, that's right...thank you. I'll hold."

Her pique only increased as he covered the receiver with one hand. "I'm holding for the doctor," he informed her. Then his attention returned to the conversation. "Hello, Dr. Payne. I'm calling for Deirdre Patten. She's one of your— yes. Yes, she is, but she's been very sick. She's lost quite a bit of weight."

He listened again, then looked at Deirdre. "He wants to know if you're throwing up regularly?"

She nodded.

"Yes," he reported. Eyes on Deirdre, he said to her, "How often, and does it last all day or is it just at certain times?"

"About ten times a day, probably," she said, looking out the window. "And yes, it's pretty constant."

She could feel his gaze boring into her, but she didn't look his way. Finally he relayed the information to the doctor. When she glanced back at him, his jaw was set and his brows were drawn together in an ominous scowl. "He wants to know how much weight you've lost."

She was silent.

Ronan raised his eyebrows.

"Thirteen pounds," she said reluctantly.

"Thirteen—!" Ronan's mouth tightened and she shrank from the flare of anger that blazed briefly in his eyes. "Thirteen pounds," he said into the handset.

"He wants to know if you're as sick as you were last

time." His eyes promised there was going to be further discussion after he hung up.

She nodded.

"She says yes," he reported to Dr. Payne. Then she listened to Ronan's side of the conversation, trying to figure out what they were discussing. "No," Ronan said. "She doesn't, but I can certainly take care of that.... Of course she can. There's no problem with that.... No, sir, I won't. All right." He held out the phone. "He wants to talk to you."

She eyed the instrument and then Ronan. Finally she took the receiver and held it to her ear. "Hello?"

"Hello, Mrs. Patten. Your husband seems very concerned about your health."

She hesitated, trying to phrase an answer that explained her situation. There was no delicate way to say it.

"Mrs. Patten? You need to take it very easy right now. I know you don't want to endanger this baby."

"Oh, no! Of course not. But, Dr. Payne, I can't just—"

"Yes, you can." The doctor's tone was warm, but firm. "I've explained to Mr. Patten that you need bed rest for the next week or so until you come in. No getting up for any reason except to go to the bathroom or my office. He doesn't seem to think that's a problem."

He isn't Mr. Patten! she wanted to shout. But her personal difficulties weren't something to burden the doctor with. "It's not," she conceded reluctantly.

"Good. Then I'll see you next week. Call me if you don't start to improve in, say, forty-eight hours, and we'll get you into the hospital for a few days until we can control that nausea."

She said goodbye to Dr. Payne and handed the telephone to Ronan, who replaced it with a less-than-gentle slam.

"*Last time?* You really got this sick before?"

"Only with Tommy," she said. "Well, with Lee, too,

but then I had the luxury of lying down whenever I needed to and I was able to control it without being hospitalized.''

"Hospitalized?'' It was almost a roar. "Are you telling me that doctor I just spoke to has put you in the hospital for this—this—sickness, before?''

She nodded, chagrined that she'd let that slip. "I'm great after the babies arrive, but I'm lousy at the incubating part.''

Ronan's expression didn't respond to her attempt to lighten the tension in the room. "I take it your husband didn't help?''

She shrugged. "He was never around.''

"So how did you manage before when you were feeling sick?''

"My mother helped out. She came and got Lee every morning and brought him back just before dinner. And she kept him at her house while I was in the hospital.''

"Why isn't she helping this time?''

She frowned at him. "Because I haven't told her yet that I'm pregnant. It isn't going to be the easiest thing in the world to explain.''

"Since when did a girl have to explain the facts of life to her mother?''

He was being deliberately obtuse, she was sure. "Since she's essentially been single for almost three years. Teenagers don't have a monopoly on shame, you know.''

Ronan stuck his hands in the back pockets of his jeans. "Were you hoping you'd miscarry?''

The question shocked her as much as the sudden change of topic. "Of course not! That's a foul thing to suggest.''

His face was set in hard lines. "A reasonable one, given the way you've let yourself get so run-down. Were you thinking of getting rid of it?''

A hard knot of rage and despair rose, almost choking her. "If I was, why would I wait until I was already half-dead?'' she said between her teeth. "And why would I tell you I was pregnant? Why would I have made an appointment for my first exam?'' It hurt that Ronan could think her capable of something so callous, and she turned her head to the wall, swallowing the sobs that tried to escape her throat.

''All right.'' Ronan walked toward the door as the boys' footsteps sounded on the stairs. ''Until that appointment, you're not getting out of this bed. I'll take care of the boys.''

''But you can't—''

''Wanna bet? I'll move into the spare bedroom. We'll talk about this more after we see the doctor.''

Ronan was in the kitchen making a chicken casserole from one of Deirdre's recipes for the evening meal. He checked out the window into the yard where he'd filled a tub of water for the boys to float toy boats in, while laughter and women's chatter could be heard floating down the stairs. The boys were fine.

Quickly he grabbed the tray he'd filled with drinks, cheese and crackers and local peaches he'd found and started up the stairs. He'd been unceremoniously kicked out of Deirdre's bedroom by Jillian and Frannie, who had been visiting for the past hour, and he was anxious to see how Deirdre was doing. She was easily exhausted, and he wasn't letting them tire her too much.

He knocked at the open door, and Jillian appeared, pulling the door wider. Ronan immediately could feel the animosity that came from her, and he knew Deirdre had told them about her pregnancy. ''I thought you might need some drinks,'' he said, ignoring Jillian and crossing the room to hand Deirdre a glass. ''And you should try to eat a few of those crackers.''

''Yes, nurse,'' Deirdre said, raising her eyebrows. ''Any other orders?''

''Now that you mention it,'' he said, ''there are. You

look tired. I think it's about time for a nap. Why don't you wrap up the visitation hour for today?''

Deirdre's face was a perfect, still cameo, her expression giving him no clue as to what she was thinking. She'd been like this for five days now, since Monday, when he'd found out she was going to have his baby. He'd suggested she call her parents so they could break the news, but she'd refused.

''I'll take care of it myself,'' she'd said.

''I'd like to be with you,'' he'd replied, irritated at the way she seemed determined to keep herself and her life totally separate from him. ''I'm involved in this situation, too.''

''I don't need your help. In any case, they're away until the end of next week, so I can't invite them to come out. And I'm not telling them over the phone.''

It was the same with her friends. ''I want to be alone with them when I tell them,'' she said, and no amount of arguing could sway her. When he saw her getting teary, he forced himself to stop snarling.

''Fine. Have it your way.'' He couldn't be gracious, but he knew when to shut up.

Now Deirdre and her friends were all looking at him as if he were a high school boy who'd wandered into the girls' locker room. ''They're leaving soon, anyway,'' she said. ''But I know my limits. I can decide for myself when I'm tired.''

''Right.'' His tone was purposely sarcastic. He knew from the color that washed up her pale cheeks that she was thinking about how poorly she'd been making decisions when he'd finally learned she was pregnant.

Jillian grabbed his arm. ''I want to talk to you a minute,'' she said aggressively. He allowed her to tow him out into the hall, realizing that Frannie had followed when she pulled the door shut behind them.

"What's up?" As if he didn't already know what bee was under her shirt.

As she led the way into a room at the far end of the hall, Jillian gave him a look designed to shrivel a man in his shoes. It damn near worked, he thought.

"She's pregnant!? What were you thinking?" she demanded. Then she held up a hand like a traffic cop. "Wait, don't answer that. I know what you were thinking. Or should I say we know what part of your anatomy you were thinking *with?*"

Frannie cast him a troubled glance, shaking her head. "This is terrible. Just terrible."

"It's not the end of the world," he said defensively. These two were acting like Deirdre had a terminal illness.

Jillian's blue eyes were very dark and very hostile. "It's not far from it, for her. Are you insane? Or just monumentally stupid? This is the last thing Deirdre needed right now."

"I know that." Ronan gritted his teeth and flexed his fingers, resisting the urge to put them around Jillian's long, tanned throat. "It didn't exactly feature in my plans, either, but I'll deal with it. And so will she."

"Deal with it how?" Frannie's face paled and she eyed Ronan with distaste. "Dee will never—"

"She's having the baby, all right? And I'm the father, and I'm not going to fade out of the picture."

"Well, let's give the boy two points for the correct answer," Jillian said.

"Knock it off, Jill," Frannie said. She looked back at Ronan. "When Dee called, she said she had two things she wanted to tell us. She says you'll tell us the second one."

Ronan took a deep breath, taken aback. He'd expected Deirdre to tell them. "I'm not a freelance journalist. I write suspense novels."

Both women looked at him expectantly. He could see the moment the truth dawned on Frannie from the way her eyes widened and her brown eyebrows shot up. "Oh, my heavens. Are you telling us you're R. J. Sullivan? *The* R. J. Sullivan?"

He nodded.

"Well, that's nice," Jillian said, not missing a beat. "At least we know you have intelligent genes to pass on to this baby." She crossed her arms. "If you're waiting for us to ask for autographs, you might want to order a few meals."

"Hold on," said Frannie. "The first time we were introduced, Dee didn't tell us who you were." Her eyes narrowed. "She didn't know, either, did she?"

"No," he admitted.

Jillian was shaking her head. "All men are selfish, self-centered jerks." She looked at Frannie. "Except for Jack on his good days."

"Dammit!" He'd had it with Deirdre's friends and their self-righteous cross-examination. "I thought you two would be a source of comfort to Deirdre. If I didn't still think that, I'd throw you out. Right now."

"Just try it." He'd never seen a woman snarl before, but Jillian was doing a good imitation.

"It must be nice to be perfect," he said. "Since it's obvious neither of you has ever made a mistake in a relationship."

There was a charged silence while the two women digested that. Jillian was the first to drop her gaze from his. "We're far from perfect," she said. "I wrote the book on broken relationships." But she was still glowering. "So what happens now?"

"What happens now," he said slowly, "is that Deirdre stays in that bed until the doctor tells her she can get up. And then—" he shrugged "—we haven't had a chance to work that out yet."

"Translation—Dee's not talking to you," Jillian said, and there was a note of glee in her tone.

"Are you staying or going?" Frannie cut right to the

heart of the matter. "What does 'not fading out of the picture' entail, exactly?"

He took a deep breath, his eyes on the steady doe eyes of Dee's friend, ignoring the hostile blonde. "It entails staying right here and helping to raise my child. Preferably married to the child's mother."

Jillian snorted.

Frannie said, "You'd be getting three children for the price of one. And two of the three are as lively as they come. Have you thought about that?"

He couldn't help it; he had to laugh. "I've thought about it," he said. "I'll probably be one step behind them all my life, but I think I can handle it."

As if talking about them had conjured them up, he heard the back door slam as the little boys came in. In the next instant, he realized one of the them was howling, and without even excusing himself, he bolted past the two women and ran down the stairs to the kitchen.

"What happened?" he demanded. Tommy was holding up one hand, sobbing wildly.

"It sorta got smashed," Lee said.

"Under what?" He dropped to the floor and took the little hand in his, realizing with relief that there was no blood.

"Well, we needed one of those logs—"

"The railroad ties? One of the railroad ties dropped on his hand?"

"On my thumb," wailed Tommy.

Ronan inspected the thumb. Sure enough, it was looking a little purple, and he suspected that the nail would be black in a few days. Rising, he took an ice pack from the freezer, wrapped it in a clean dish towel and picked up the crying child with quick, economical motions, settling into the rocking chair near the fireplace.

"Let's get some ice on that," he said, rubbing the little boy's back. "I bet that hurts, but I don't think you broke

anything.'' He cuddled the child, enjoying the feel of the
sturdy little body in his arms as Tommy's sobs died away
to occasional sniffles.

"So we don't hafta go to the hospital?" Lee sounded
almost disappointed.

"Don't think so," Ronan said. "Unless you want me to
clobber you for destroying your mother's flower bed for
that railroad tie.''

Lee gave him a sheepish grin. "Nope." Then he bright-
ened, casting Ronan a sly glance from under his lashes. "I
think we can fix it after supper. If you can lift the railroad
log.''

A sound made Ronan glance up, and he realized he'd
forgotten all about Deirdre's friends. Frannie stood in the
hallway door. She had a small smile on her face, and as
her eyes met his, he realized there was approval in their
depths. "Dee's napping," she informed him. "We're leaving now…Daddy.''

Two weeks came and went. For the first week she did
little but sleep, and eat the meals Ronan and the boys
brought to her room. As she'd expected, simply getting
enough rest helped her body to resist the nausea she experienced every time she was pregnant. She decided she
hated women who breezed through their pregnancies without one single, solitary day of queasiness.

During the second week she began to chafe at the re-
strictions, but Ronan wouldn't even agree to her coming
downstairs until after the doctor gave her permission to do
so. He did, finally, gather a list of items from her workshop
and bring them to her so that she could do a little bit of
work by hand, although he watched her like a hawk, re-
minding her to nap practically every fifteen minutes.

He took her back to the doctor the following Thursday.
She'd dressed and was sitting on the side of the bed, waiting for him to help her downstairs. She could have done it

herself, but the grief he would give her just wasn't worth it. And, though she'd lie naked on an anthill before she'd admit it to him, taking a shower and dressing for the appointment had tired her out.

She heard him coming up the steps, and when he entered the room, she rose, wondering what he was thinking as he looked at her. When she had looked in the bathroom mirror earlier—practically the only place she could be alone without Ronan checking up on her—the face that met her eyes had lost its gaunt pallor, and she thought she was starting to resemble herself again.

And Ronan…Ronan looked as good to her as he always did. His dark hair was slicked down with water from the shower she'd heard him taking earlier, and his face and arms were more deeply tanned than before—probably from chasing Lee and Tommy all over the farm. He was wearing khaki-colored pants and an ivory shirt with the sleeves rolled up, and he looked so casually elegant she wondered how she ever had thought he was a down-and-out journalist struggling to make ends meet.

He came toward her, unsmiling, his golden eyes intent, and she knew he was assessing her, a habit he'd acquired in the past few weeks that drove her crazy. She hated feeling like an invalid who needed to be watched over.

"I'm ready," she said as he stopped before her. He was close, and she had to tilt her head back to look at him. A mistake. He was standing so near she was afraid he would think she was inviting his kiss. But he didn't betray any such thoughts, if they'd even entered his head.

"All right. Let's go," was all he said. But he didn't offer her his arm. Instead, he bent and caught her behind the knees and the shoulders, lifting her up into his arms.

"Ronan!" She clutched at his shoulders. "Put me down. I told you yesterday I can walk. You'll hurt yourself."

"I won't hurt myself, and you're not walking anywhere

until you get the doc's say-so,'' he told her in a firm voice as he started out of the room.

The heat of his body all along the side that was against him felt so good that she couldn't bring herself to argue anymore. Too good. *This is a man who lied to you,* she reminded herself, *a man who didn't trust you enough to share the truth about his life. A man whose chief concern now is the baby you're carrying.*

A man who doesn't love you.

But as much as she hated it, the simple truth was that she still wanted him, still cared...still loved him, even though his duplicity still seared her heart with pain every time she thought about it.

He smelled of some wonderful cologne. The scent seemed concentrated at the base of his throat, where a few curling hairs peeped from the neck of the shirt, and with a heavy sigh that released the angst warring within her, she laid her head against his shoulder in surrender, breathing deeply of him.

Her fingers wanted to play with the hair brushing his collar, and she had to force herself not to touch as he carried her down the steps. His jaw was just above eye level, and she drank in the sight of the smooth, tanned skin, freshly shaved, that stretched over the strong bones. Warmth skittered through her abdomen, and her chest felt tight. Why, of all the men in the world, did he have whatever it was that made her literally forget everything and long to lie down beneath him? It was a good thing that she didn't react this way to every man that came along. She just wished she had a little more control around this one.

At the bottom of the steps he paused and looked down at her. His eyes darkened to the deep amber of awareness, and beneath her hands, she felt the strong muscles of his shoulders tense. Time slowed, braked to a gentle halt around them. His gaze drifted down to her mouth, and she felt the pull, as if he were willing her mouth to his. She took a deep breath, unable to take her eyes from his face.

"I don't want to kiss you." His voice was a deep rumble that vibrated through her.

Shock widened her eyes, and before she could catch it, snatch back the hurt in her voice, she said, "Why not?"

"Because." He was still looking at her mouth as he spoke, and she couldn't fathom how that single small thing could make her whole body quiver with sexual excitement. "I can't kiss you without losing track of every ounce of common sense I have."

A warmth spread through her, even though his words had nothing to do with feeling, only with his physical preoccupation with her body. "I thought maybe it was just me."

"Nope." Her mouth was practically tingling where his gaze touched her. She tightened her arms the merest fraction, tilting her head up even more, and with a long, slow exhalation of breath he took her lips.

It wasn't the ravaging invasion, the frantic, devouring need that had always been between them, but a softer, sweeter meeting that offered her passion while promising a light hand, a gentle touch. His tongue curled around hers, then drew away to outline her lips, explore the contours of her mouth, and she slid both hands up the warm, firm flesh of his throat to cradle his cheeks in her palms as he kissed her, kissed her and kissed her again. Her entire body was shaking in his arms when he finally lifted his mouth and released hers.

"We have to talk." His eyes searched hers at close range. "Later."

"Yes," she whispered. At the very least they needed to discuss arrangements for the baby. Beyond that…beyond that, she couldn't think. She loved him. Even knowing he didn't love her, was only pampering her for the sake of the child she carried, she loved him so much she ached with it. Her world would collapse in on itself if he left, she knew.

But she also knew that unless she could unlock the door within her that had slammed shut the day she'd stood listening to that answering machine, she couldn't keep on the way things were. Oh, God, she was so confused.

The doctor was pleased with her. She'd gained weight, and the nausea was far less threatening now that she was getting enough rest. To her relief, she was given permission to be on her feet again, as long as she rested three times a day and didn't begin to throw up again.

That evening, after Ronan brought her home from the doctor, she begged him to let her stay downstairs. As she'd anticipated, he balked, telling her she needed to rest after the trip to town. Reduced to begging, she told him she was so tired of floral wallpaper and the matching bedspread she could scream, and he relented, letting her recline on the couch in her living room.

While he went into the kitchen to start some spaghetti for dinner, she eyed the door to her workroom at the front of the house, wondering if she could sneak in there for a few minutes. She'd been away from everything but the little handwork she'd been able to do in bed, and she was dying to get back to work. Fortunately, she'd been well ahead of schedule, due to all those miserable, sleepless nights, but soon she needed to wrap up a few orders and get them out, or the money wouldn't come *in*, and that was going to be crucial in the next few months.

"Don't even think about it."

She turned from her contemplation to see Ronan standing in the doorway to the kitchen. His lips were pressed firmly together, his hair was disheveled and his eyes drilled into her with a deep intensity that made her flush as if she were guilty of something.

"Think of what?"

"You're not going into that workroom until tomorrow at the earliest," he said. "And then only for very short periods of time. I'll be glad to bring you anything you want to work on.''

"I've finished all the handwork I can do right now," she said in frustration. "I need to get back to my machine. My customers are going to start wondering what's going on if I don't get a few of the outstanding orders done soon."

"I'll explain to your customers what's going on if anybody asks," he said calmly. "You're having a rough pregnancy and have been unable to work."

"You mean I wasn't allowed to work."

"Stop sulking." He walked to the edge of the sofa where she lay and eased down to sit beside her. His body warmed her hip where they were pressed together, and she was all too aware of the compelling beauty of his chiseled features as he leaned over her. "You heard the doctor as clearly as I did."

"Yes, but it's not as if I have to climb in and out of a car and work on my feet for eight hours a day. Even an hour here or there would help." She paused. What the heck—why was she worrying about what he thought at this point? "I need the money."

Ronan hesitated. It was rare to see him unsure, so rare that it caught her off guard. She should have seized the opportunity to press her case, but she was caught in the depths of his eyes, drawn into a wordless exchange that had nothing to do with work.

"Stop worrying about money," he said finally. "I'll take care of anything that comes up."

"I don't want you to. It's important to me that I take care of my family myself. I already owe you more than I can hope to repay unless I win the lottery." She heard the bitterness in her voice, but darn it, she felt bitter about the way she'd been so blind.

"In case it's escaped you, we're going to be sharing a family soon." He smoothed the hair away from her forehead. "You're making this money thing a bigger deal than it has to be."

With very little provocation, she could turn her head and take off a few of his fingers. Shaking off his hand, she said through her teeth, "I will never be dependent on a man again."

"It's not dependency!" His voice rose. "You're the polar opposite of my damned ex-wife, do you know that? She was more than happy to be dependent on my money." He laughed harshly. "She was even happier once she was independent again with my money."

Deirdre's dark brows drew together, and her green eyes were stormy. "I can be independent without your money, so thanks but no thanks for the noble gesture."

"It wasn't a gesture," he shouted. "I meant it! Men and women have been forming partnerships for centuries— what's so wrong with us doing the same?"

"We aren't a partnership." Her voice grew as loud as his. "We're one person who trusted another, and one person who couldn't be bothered to share his real life with her!"

"You're never going to let me forget that, are you?" He flung his hands in the air as he propelled himself off the couch.

Her heart hurt. "How can I, when I can't forget it myself?" she whispered.

"If I could live this summer over again, I can think of about a million things I'd do differently." He turned from where he'd stopped on the other side of the room and a shadow passed across his face. "I meant to tell you about my work. But the opportunity kept slipping away. I was going to tell you the day we went to the Harbor...." His eyes met hers, and in an instant she was catapulted back in time, swamped in the sensual haze of that lazy day, when sex filled the air like a water-laden towel and she learned what it truly meant to have a man worship your body. She swallowed, and he went on. "After that, you know there wasn't really a good time."

And she had to admit he was right. Once the nightmare with the boys had begun, there was no time for personal concerns. And the next day…the next day, she'd taken those stupid cookies over to his apartment.

"Deirdre, I don't want to hide my life from you."

She swallowed. "Your life isn't really any of my business, Ronan. Except in terms of how you plan to fit into this baby's life."

His lips thinned, but he didn't say anything. The silence stretched and sagged between them and she knew he was regretting this whole mess. What for him had been a few casual encounters had been far more to her. And now they were linked forever by the life they'd made together.

He stood, pushing away from the couch. "I have to get that spaghetti sauce before it burns." But he made no move to go. "After dinner, after the boys are in bed, I'm taking you over to see my apartment. That way you can't imagine all the things you think I'm hiding."

"We can't leave the boys," she protested.

"The boys will be fine for the few minutes we'll be gone," he said. "I'll put Murphy in the hallway between their rooms and you can carry the intercom monitor along so that if they wake up, we'll hear them."

He had it all worked out. And she could see from the expression on his face that further protests would fall on deaf ears. She certainly hoped this baby didn't inherit its father's stubbornness.

Nine

Deirdre wouldn't let him carry her to his apartment later in the evening, and he figured he was pushing his luck just to get her over there at all. He was anxious to show it to her, not only the apartment improvements he'd made, but his work. The work station he'd set up. The galleys on his desk, the cover flats…he wanted her to understand his life.

As she slowly mounted the stairs, he hovered behind her, ready to grab for her if she seemed unwell. Finally she turned and thrust out her arm, palm against his shoulder, holding him back. "Stop crowding me," she said. "I feel fine as long as I don't rush or overdo it."

He grinned reluctantly. "You know, when I first met you, you seemed like such a sweet little thing. But you have a stubborn streak a mile wide. I hope this baby doesn't have it, too."

They'd reached the landing at the top of the steps and he inserted his key in the lock.

"I'm stubborn? Look who's talking." She cast him a

disdainful glance. "We're standing here because you wouldn't take no for an answer, buddy. So don't talk to me about stubborn!"

Sheesh! This wasn't an argument he could win, judging from the aggressive tone in her voice. So instead of answering, he swung open the door and motioned for her to precede him into the room.

Slowly, like one stepping into a lake of dark water without knowing the depth, she moved forward. One step, then two.

He closed the door and stepped up to her side, surveying the room through her eyes. He'd done a hell of a fine redecorating job, if he did say so himself. "Well, what do you think?"

She didn't answer. Her gaze swept from one side to the other, seeing the expensive equipment, the paneling and carpet, the lighting and the nice little porcelain sink with its gleaming brass fixtures in the kitchenette.

"So. Do you like it?" He was anxious for her reaction, and that bothered him. Never before had he needed another person's stamp of approval to validate his decisions. Even in his writing he'd never compromised, simply wrote what pleased him and left his agent to worry about how and where—and if—it would sell.

"It's beautiful," she said. "You've done a lovely job." But there was a flat, distant quality to her voice. "You have to tell me how much the improvements cost, and I'll set up a payment schedule to reimburse you."

"Didn't we just have this conversation?" He struggled for a light tone. "I didn't expect you to pay for this when I did it. In fact, you agreed to let me do whatever I wanted to the place, as I recall."

"Yes, but—"

"And this is what I wanted."

"You're missing the point. On purpose."

"I know." Maybe he could charm her out of her pique.

''Come over here. I want to show you my setup. It doesn't look like much, but I have everything I need for my writing all right here. Separate lines for fax, phone and e-mail, a computer that's not hooked up to the internet where I do my actual writing.''

She had picked up a green glass paperweight his mother had given him after he sold his first book. The myriad shades of green swirling and slicing through the glass represented the forty shades of the green of Ireland. His mother was proud of that heritage and didn't hesitate to remind him of it at any opportunity. It struck him that his mother and hers would have a high old time together discussing their favorite topic.

''This is something I miss,'' she said wistfully, running a fingertip over his beloved P.C. ''Nelson got the computer, and I haven't replaced it yet. I need to do it soon, though. The boys are old enough to be getting accustomed to a keyboard.''

As she turned away and prowled around the room, examining things here and there, he looked at the rounded curve of her breast and her slender hips. She still was not showing any evidence of her pregnancy, but she was filling out her clothing more like he remembered. Her hair was loose, the way he loved it, and he fought the urge to go to her and plunge his fingers into the thick, curling mass, to drag her against him and press those sweet, yielding hips to his. But he knew they needed to get back to the house. He wasn't any more comfortable leaving the boys than she was, even if they were just next door.

The boys. She was a great mother. She never gave herself a thought without relating it to how it would affect her children.

Children. A sudden flash of intuition swept through him. She would be doing that for his child soon.

The thought brought with it a humbling sense of responsibility, and he allowed the plan that had been tumbling through his head for days to coalesce into a firm course of action. She was going to marry him. There was no way he was going to let a child of his grow up without a father and a family. Besides, she loved him. She'd said so.

Aloud, he said, "I've been letting them fool around with my laptop a little bit. But I'll make arrangements to have this one moved over to the house now. Where do you think we should put it?"

She turned and looked at him, a puzzled frown digging two little vertical dents into the space between her eyebrows. "Why on earth would you move your computer into my house?"

"I'll be living there," he pointed out. "I figured we should just go ahead and get married."

She let her hand drop from his computer and turned to look at him. Her eyes resembled the shades of color in his paperweight, shifting and changing so fast he couldn't discern her thoughts. "Married?"

He shrugged. Keep it casual. Act as if it's no big deal. "You're pregnant with my baby. We ought to give it my name."

She simply stared at him.

Crossing the room, he took her hands in his. "I think we should get married, Deirdre. Your sons need a real father in their lives. You're going to want to spend more time with this baby once it's born, and I don't want you worrying about working to make ends meet." She didn't say a word, and he couldn't read her eyes. He supposed she needed more convincing, and he put a hand to her breast, lightly rubbing his thumb against the very tip of her nipple until he felt the little bud spring to firm life. "Our bodies have already agreed that we're a good match."

She closed her eyes, and he continued to caress her as he spoke again. "I don't mind that the decision was forced on me. In fact, the more I think about marriage, the better I like the idea."

Her hand lifted, settled around his wrist, and after another moment she pulled his hand away from her breast. Her eyes opened, smoky green with unfulfilled desire. "What do you mean, the decision was forced on you?" Her tone was merely curious.

"You know," he said. "This whole deal with you getting pregnant."

"I don't want you to feel forced into marrying me." Her eyes had cleared. They were strangely cool, and the first warning of impending danger grabbed him by the throat.

"It isn't exactly like that," he protested. Inspiration struck. "You told me you loved me. If you love me, there's no problem."

"I guess there isn't, from your perspective," she said slowly.

She was agreeing! He pushed on, anxious to get this behind them so they could get on to more important things, like baby names and his travel schedule. "I can have my lawyer get a prenuptial agreement together in a day or so. We could probably get married by the end of the month. How does that sound?"

She didn't answer him, and he put a finger beneath her chin, tipping her face up to his. But she stepped back, out of his hands, linking her fingers together in front of her. "It all sounds very practical, Ronan. You've thought of almost everything." She took a deep breath. "I'm going to pass on the proposal. Thanks, but no thanks, as they say."

The vise around his throat tightened. She couldn't say no! "Why?" he managed to croak.

She regarded him steadily, and a single tear welled up in her eye and spilled down her cheek, slipping into the corner of her mouth. Her tongue came out and whisked over the shining trail it had made, and her lip quivered, but she didn't respond.

"It's the prenup, isn't it?" he said. "You don't want to

sign anything that might prevent you from keeping half my assets if we divorce.''

Her checks paled. She was silent.

''That's it, isn't it?'' He crossed his arms and shrugged. ''It's good business. I have no intention of watching you walk away with half my fortune if we divorce. Not that I think that will happen,'' he added hastily.

She shook her head, and there was a sad, haunted quality to her eyes when she raised them to his again. ''I didn't say no because of that. But now that you mention it, a prenuptial contract would be a problem for me. I don't believe in entering a marriage with an escape hatch. I would never leave you.''

''How do I know that? You left Nelson.'' He knew it was a crummy thing to say, but she had turned this whole thing around and put him on the defensive. Why was this such a big deal?

Any hints of color that remained in her face had drained away, and she put a hand on the back of a chair. He reached forward, sensing she needed support, but she backed away from his grasp. ''I would never leave you,'' she repeated, ''because you would never cause me to fear for my safety or my children's. You're not a Nelson.''

''So why won't you marry me?'' It was a bellow of frustration.

''If you don't know why, there's no point in continuing this conversation,'' she said softly.

He was too stunned to move. As he stood like a stupid stone, still turning her words over and over in his head without having any sense of their meaning, she turned and slipped out of the apartment, pocketing her baby monitor as she went. ''Don't follow me down. I'll be fine.''

He couldn't have followed her if he'd wanted to. He didn't believe it. She had refused to marry him. A great yawning hole of blackness swirling with questions and unfinished thoughts prevented him from going after her and demanding an explanation. His proposal was sensible, right down to the prenuptial agreement. Surely she could see that. And if it wasn't a prenup that bothered her, what was wrong? Why had she said no?

Panic welled up. He couldn't imagine a life without her. He'd gotten comfortable living with a family a whole lot quicker than he'd ever have believed, especially with two little hellions like Lee and Tommy around. But he'd liked the way they seemed to need him. He liked knowing that Deirdre was just a few steps away in another room. He liked everything about being part of a family.

Well, okay, so he didn't particularly enjoy the cooking end of the deal. But she probably didn't, either. It just came with the territory.

And, even though he had never gotten the chance to try it out, he knew that he would like sharing a bed with her every night. Actually sleeping with her cuddled in his arms, the way they'd dozed during that afternoon at the harbor. All night. Even after the wild, runaway desire that she stirred in him had been slaked, he still had wanted to hold her. Had needed it, he corrected himself.

He'd never felt that way about Sonja. In fact, he'd known going into his first marriage that he needed a certain amount of space. He hadn't particularly liked her hovering over him, always reaching for his hand, wanting to sit in his lap. He really hadn't liked the way she'd twined herself around him at night—he'd found it hard to get a decent night's sleep with another person right in his face.

But he didn't mind any of those things with Deirdre. In fact, he wanted to touch her as much as she did him, casually renewing their bond with the intimate contacts, the way he'd seen other couples do. He loved the way she felt snuggled into his lap, and recently he'd caught himself waking from sleep reaching for her, before he remembered she was in another bed in a room down the hall. He deserved a gold medal for resisting the voice in his head that told him to walk down the hall and slide into bed with her, just pull her against him and sink into the sweet oblivion of sleep with her in his arms, where she belonged.

As he slowly locked the apartment and left the stable, he knew he wouldn't get any sleep tonight. And it wasn't just because he had a bedroom down the hall from hers. He'd been blindly refusing to acknowledge his feelings for weeks, but he couldn't put it off any longer.

He cared for Deirdre more than he could remember ever caring for another woman in his life. If he wasn't such a chicken, he'd even say…he loved her. *He loved her!* He wasn't sure when the all-consuming passion he knew whenever he was around her had transformed itself into a feeling that endured whether or not she was nearby, but he suspected it had been about three seconds after he'd laid eyes on her in that grocery store. Hell, he'd been half in love with his fantasy Deirdre already. The real thing had been so much more…more *real* that he'd been reeling from its impact ever since.

He loved her. He needed her to complete his life, to complete him.

But she'd walked away.

With the sudden wisdom always conferred by hindsight, he knew what she'd needed to hear from him tonight. She hadn't needed lists of practical reasons or personal advantages.

If you don't know why, there's no point in continuing this conversation.

How could he have missed the pain in those soft words? He'd even hammered the hurt in deeper when he'd used *her* love for *him* in his damned list.

She needed his love. She had needed to hear him say the words, the words he'd been resisting even thinking…and he'd missed the opportunity. So how in hell could he convince her to give him another chance?

* * *

The next day she acted as friendly and normal as if the wrenching conversation last night had never occurred. Although Ronan noticed she didn't quite meet his eyes when she looked his way. Instead, her gaze bounced off his temple and skittered away. He practically had to tie his tongue down to keep from saying anything about marriage. Or love.

He could feel his patience being whittled away and he forced himself to grab it and hang on with both hands. In just a short while, they'd have time to talk. Deirdre's mother had returned from her trip and was coming to get the boys this evening for an overnight visit. Deirdre hadn't told her mother about her pregnancy yet; he knew she'd planned to do it tomorrow evening, when her parents were coming for dinner. She'd still wanted to tell them alone quietly, but he'd told her he would crash the meeting if she didn't include him. The speed with which she'd capitulated told him how much she needed his support, even if she hadn't said it.

But would she still allow him to be there now?

Mrs. Halleran showed up while he was clearing the dinner dishes. Deirdre had been sitting tensely by a front window watching for her mother. As the car came down the lane she hustled the boys outside. Her mother probably thought it was peculiar of her daughter not to invite her in for a chat, since she'd been away for two weeks, but Deirdre might have claimed her work as an excuse. And they'd have plenty of time to talk tomorrow evening…though he doubted the Hallerans' trip would be the big topic.

As the car pulled out of the driveway, he drained the sink and hung up the dishcloth. His pulse felt quick and his breath was shallow, as if he'd just received a shot of adrenaline. Now. Now he could tell her how mistaken he'd been last night. Now he could—hey!

Deirdre was climbing into her car.

He raced out the door like he was still a sprinter for his

old high school team, reaching the side of the car just as she turned the key. Over the low growl of the engine, he demanded, "Where are you going?"

"To the corner store." She glanced at his temple again. "I know I haven't driven in a while. I'll be careful."

"The doctor didn't tell you you could drive."

"He didn't tell me I couldn't," she said. "I just felt too lousy before."

"When you come back—"

"I've been thinking—" They both started to speak at once.

Then they both stopped. Ronan gestured impatiently. "You first."

She nodded. "Ronan, there's no need for you to stay in the house tonight since the boys aren't here. And I've been thinking—I'm feeling well enough to deal with breakfast and bedtime next week, so I won't need you to stay with us anymore. If you don't mind, I'd still appreciate the help with lunch and dinner." She smiled nervously, meeting his eyes for the first time. "And laundry. Now, what were you going to say?"

She was kicking him out! He searched for words, but couldn't remember what he'd started to say. "You can't kick me out."

She winced. "I didn't really think of it as kicking you out. I appreciate everything you've done to help." She swallowed. "I know I was ungracious at first, but it meant a lot to me. I do want this baby, and I know you do, too. We don't have to be in a rush to start working out the parenting arrangements—I know your schedule isn't very regular, so I'm willing to be flexible about the times you take the baby."

"That isn't what I want to discuss." He knew his voice was abrupt, but he couldn't help it. She seemed to be one step ahead of him on the wrong road all the time, and he was damn tired of it. "When you get back from the store," he said in a menacing tone, "we are going to sit down and talk about our relationship. About you and me. And you are going to listen to what I have to say before you work out any more plans in your head."

She hung her head for a moment as if she were incredibly weary. When she raised it again, there was troubled determination in her face. "We pretty much said anything necessary last night, Ronan. And I'm not into dragging my feelings out to be stomped on again and again." Her lower lip trembled, and she bit down on it fiercely. "When I get back from the store, I'm going into my workroom." She put the car in gear and slowly started to move. "And I expect you to be moved out of my house."

Out of her house? Not a chance, he thought, watching her car negotiate the potholes in the lane. All right. Fine. Let her drive away. He was going to take a walk. A long walk. And then they were going to talk. Whether or not she liked it.

She loved him, dammit! And she wasn't walking away from what they had just because he'd been too dumb to figure it out for a while.

He whistled for Murphy, who was lounging on the porch, watching him with sleepy eyes. At the first hint of encouragement, Murphy leaped up and barreled off the steps toward him.

Ronan bent to scratch the thick-furred ears. "At least somebody around here is glad to see me." The words sounded pretty pitiful, even to him.

She was just getting out of the car with the quart of milk she didn't really need when the sound of a car's tires crunching down the lane reached her ears. She frowned, straining to see in the darkening evening. She wasn't expecting anyone.

It was a light-colored sedan of some kind, she could see that as it crested the ridge. And as it came toward her, closer and closer, a thick ball of apprehension lodged in her stomach.

It was Nelson.

Her mind raced as he drew the car to a halt and stepped out. What was he doing? How had he found her?

Thank God the boys weren't here. Thank God. And in her rearview mirror, she'd seen Ronan take Murphy with him when he'd started to walk back across the field earlier. A good thing, considering how Murphy felt about her ex-husband. It seemed luck was with her. So maybe, just maybe, she could get rid of Nelson before anything awful happened.

Ronan. She stifled the wave of longing. He didn't love her. Or he'd have told her so last night. And despite the desire to simply say, ''Yes!'' to his carefully-outlined stupid proposal of marriage, with its insulting conditions, she'd walked away. She couldn't live with him for the rest of her life, receiving only his physical adoration, sharing this child and maybe more, without her heart wilting and shriveling into nothing, without becoming bitter and mean. And she loved him too much to do that to him.

''Deirdre! You're looking well.''

A shiver of revulsion rippled through her, raising goose bumps on her arms and making the back of her neck prickle uncomfortably. She wasn't afraid of Nelson, exactly, though she probably should be. It was more of the back-away-from-a-really-foul-odor variety feeling she was experiencing. ''Thank you,'' she said quietly. ''You know you shouldn't be here.''

He waved a hand through the air in dismissive contempt. ''So says some dumb judge who doesn't even know us.'' He stepped closer, and she realized there was something strange in his eyes. Something unsure. ''I want—I'd like to talk to you for a few minutes. If you don't mind.''

This new obsequious deference was as threatening to her as his normal dominant demeanor. At least then she'd known what he was thinking as he'd shouted at her. "All right," she said cautiously.

He started around her, toward the house.

"No," she said, surreptitiously checking her watch. "We can talk here." She didn't want him befouling her home with his presence. Her life now was Nelson-free and she wanted to keep it that way. She didn't want to picture him sitting in her kitchen.

Her ex-husband turned around, and she read surprise in his lifted eyebrows. She rarely had stood up to him in the past. But all he said was "All right." He backed up and leaned against her car, drawing out a cigarette. "So. How've you been?"

"Fine," she said impatiently. "What do you want?"

"Nothing much." His eyes were narrowed against the cigarette's smoke as he exhaled.

She moved away from the acrid cloud of smoke without speaking.

"I'm getting married again," he said abruptly.

That was a surprise. "I didn't realize there was anyone you were that serious with. Congratulations." Part of her wanted to jump for joy at the notion that he'd stopped obsessing about her. But another side whispered dire warnings. Married, Nelson might look like a more stable parent to a judge. What if he challenged her for custody? She was single—and pregnant with another man's child. Any lawyer worth his salt would have a field day with her morals.

"Her name's Nita," he said. "I'd like to introduce her to the boys on Sunday. I think you and the boys will really like her."

Maybe so, if she could get Nelson to behave like this all the time. "What, exactly, did you have in mind?"

"I'd like to bring her out here."

"Which brings up another point," she said. "How did you find out where I lived?"

But Nelson's attention was suddenly fixed on the hilltop field. "Who's that?"

She turned, her heart sinking. She had prayed she could get rid of Nelson before Ronan returned. "It's my tenant," she said, identifying the figure. "I've rented out an apartment."

"Hmm." Nelson turned and surveyed the other buildings on her property, then began to stroll toward the stable, which stood with its heavy door open wide.

"Wait!" she said. "Where are you going?"

"I want to talk to you without being interrupted," he said.

"We could talk in your car," she said hopefully, reluctantly trailing behind him.

"This'll do fine." Nelson reached behind her and pulled the door of the stable shut, and she jumped in alarm, stepping back from him. Her movement drew his gaze, and a strange expression twisted his lips for a moment. He took a long drag on his cigarette, exhaling the smoke toward the ceiling. "Look," he said. "I've been a jerk, I admit it. I treated you like a slave when we were married. And taking the kids down to the cabin wasn't a smart thing to do. I don't know what I was thinking…I've really missed them since they stopped coming with me on Sundays."

A tiny piece of her heart thawed. This man had many, many flaws, in her eyes, but this was the first time she'd ever heard him sound as if he cared for Lee and Tommy. While she wasn't about to leave her children alone with him, she knew it could only help them to have Nelson take an interest in them. And if that happened, she would live with her dislike. "I don't see any problem with you and your fiancée coming out on Sunday," she said, just as a ferocious barking began, some distance away. Murphy had scented his nemesis.

Nelson jolted, turning toward the door with a fearful expression. "I didn't know the dog was out. Can he get in here?"

"I don't think so," she said. "I'll check the door to the paddock. It should be closed, but you'll feel better if you're certain."

Nelson followed her closely as she walked to the back of the structure to check the big door. It was as tightly closed as she'd expected, and a padlocked bar on the outside added double security. "There," she said, turning to him. "You won't have to see Murphy again. My tenant can put him in the house until you leave."

The barking grew closer and they both paused, listening. Then a heavy body thudded against the door at the far end of the stable. Murphy was growling: she had no doubt that he remembered Nelson from their last encounter. He ran around the barn and vicious snarling accompanied a brief, futile scratching at the door. Then the dog's claws could be heard against the wall beneath the high windows.

"I thought you said your tenant would take care of him," Nelson said. Even through the gloom she could see sweat beading his face. A wave of sympathy, totally unexpected, rolled over her. Poor man. He'd made a huge mess of his life, lost his children, driven away his wife and earned the undying hatred of the dog outside. She felt blessed in comparison.

"He should be along any minute," she said soothingly. To get his mind off the dog, she said, "Tell me about…Nita? That's an unusual name—" She broke off. What was that smell? Almost like…smoke! It was smoke—there was a fire in the barn!

She wheeled and looked back toward the front of the stable, where the stairs led up to Ronan's apartment. To her horror, thick black smoke was rolling through the dark barn. She could even see some orange, licking streaks of flame, and she realized they couldn't hope to get out the door at that end—and this one was locked from the outside.

"Ronan!" she screamed. "Ronan, there's a fire in the stable. We're locked inside." Already the smoke was slipping its silent, deadly way into her lungs, and she began to cough. Beside her, Nelson was moaning and coughing. She grabbed at his arm. "Get down!"

He resisted her and she grabbed at him again. "Nelson! Get down. It's easier to breathe near the floor."

"It's not going to matter," he said. "We're going to be burned to death."

She could feel the heat rippling outward. Wildly she looked around, but there was nothing that would help. Both fire extinguishers were located near the other door and everything else—everything else, except the concrete floor on which they were crouched, was highly flammable.

"Deirdre? Where are you? Deirdre!"

Through Murphy's now-frantic barking she heard Ronan's voice, and she almost sobbed with relief. "Ronan! We're around back." She was seized by another deep, ugly cough.

"Cover your faces!" They obeyed without comprehension and a moment later a thick board—part of the fence outside, she realized—shattered the closest window. She could barely see it, and the heat gave a hungry surge forward as it found fresh air to feed on, searing the backs of her legs. She screamed.

And then Ronan was there. He scooped her from the floor, shouting, "Come on," to Nelson, and in a single smooth move, hoisted her through the window. Even in his haste, he was careful to be sure he set her on the hay bales he'd dragged over to reach the window.

She rolled off the hay to make room for the men, turning to look back as she did, but no one followed her down. Smoke was pouring from the broken opening now. Murphy, jumping anxiously around the foot of the pile, grabbed her shirt firmly in his big teeth and dragged her away. She shook free of him but he simply grabbed her arm gently but firmly in his mouth and she realized her dog wasn't letting her go any closer.

"Ronan!" she cried out. He appeared in the window, and she could see that he had his arm around Nelson. Nelson appeared to be barely conscious, and Ronan had to help him as he struggled to get his arms through the window. But as he caught sight of the dog waiting with her, he hesitated. Murphy leaped to his feet, barking, and suddenly Nelson shoved himself backward, tearing at Ronan's arm. The unexpected resistance caught Ronan off guard. Nelson turned and plunged away, back into the inferno behind them.

"Ronan!" She called out again. Visibility inside the barn had to be zilch; he couldn't hope to locate Nelson if he wasn't close by. Ronan hesitated—and disappeared from the window. All she could see was one hand desperately gripping the sill. She moaned, covering her mouth with her hand, holding her breath. Then he reappeared, pulling himself slowly up and out. Murphy, impatient with Ronan's pace, leaped onto the pile of hay and fastened his teeth in Ronan's shirt. The big dog's muscles strained as he dragged the man's heavy weight forward until he fell free of the window, groaning and coughing.

She sprang forward, aiding the dog as fire sirens began to squeal in the distance. Haunches flexing powerfully, Murphy steadily pulled Ronan away from the hay. He didn't stop pulling until they were at the far end of the paddock and she finally said, "Enough, Murph. *Enough!*"

And as the exhausted dog dropped to the ground beside them, the roof of the stable fell in with a whoosh and a muted roar that chilled her as deeply as the smoke had invaded her lungs.

Ten

Deirdre threw such a fit about staying in the hospital overnight that Ronan told the doctor he'd watch her like a hawk if she could be discharged the following day. He hadn't been kept for observation, she complained, and he'd inhaled at least as much smoke as she had, received just as many minor burns.

"I'm not pregnant, either," Ronan had said, crossing his arms as he leaned against the door of her hospital room. Lee and Tommy were still with her mother, whom Ronan had restrained from rushing to the hospital; Deirdre didn't want the boys to see her in a hospital bed. And she was terrified that they might overhear some unguarded conversation. She wanted them to be in their own home, surrounded by familiar things, when she broke the news of their father's death.

The fire and rescue workers had pulled Nelson's body—or what remained of it—from the pile of smoking rubble as soon as the heat had died back enough. She'd spent the time in the hospital grieving for the father of her sons from the point of view of her sons, and carefully thinking through how to explain Nelson's death to the children.

She was so thankful that Nelson's last conversation with her had been a positive one. It would be such a relief not to have to lie to them. She sighed, rolling her head against the back of her seat when Ronan turned his truck off the main road and onto the lane that led home. As they bumped up and over the ridge and started down the other side, the farm spread out before them. And like a great blackened wart on vital, healthy skin, the charred remnants of the stable lay right in the middle of it all. Yellow police tape barred observers from wandering too close.

After all, a man had died in there.

She wasn't aware of making any sound, but Ronan reached across the seat and took her hand, linking his fingers with hers. "You okay?"

"Yes." It was a near whisper, and she cleared her throat, conscious of the last effects of smoke-inhalation. "Seeing it is...hard."

"I know." He braked the truck in front of the house and came around to lift her down from the seat, and they walked forward for a closer view of the devastation that had nearly taken their lives, too.

Ronan stood just behind her, his big hands resting on her shoulders, thumbs absently brushing back and forth across her nape. It had to be hard for him, she knew. He'd lost all his equipment, with much of his livelihood tied up in the computers that had been destroyed.

"What will you do about your book? And your screen-play?"

She felt him shrug. "I had saved most of it on a floppy in the truck," he said. "It's a habit, to keep two copies in separate locations. I've done it every day for years." His voice dropped. "Now I know why."

She shook her head, amusement and relief touching the

edges of her melancholy. "What a weird thing to do. But I'm very glad you do. I guarantee nothing survived that fire undamaged."

Silence fell.

Finally Ronan spoke. "Why? In the name of God, why wouldn't he let me help him out? He could be standing here today." His tone was low and anguished. "He just—just dove back into the smoke and I couldn't find him." He sighed. "I should have gone farther from the window, but I couldn't see a thing and I was afraid if I let go of the sill, I'd never find it again."

"You did everything you could. Nelson's death isn't your fault." She raised both her hands to cover his and a deep sigh of sorrow escaped her. "Actually, I think I'm partly to blame."

"What?" Ronan turned her to face him. "That's ridiculous. If you hadn't been screaming, I'd never have found you in time. I was still circling the front when I heard you."

"It's not ridiculous." She sniffed and leaned her forehead against his chest, speaking to the ground. "I encouraged his fear of Murphy. He was such a nervous wreck that he probably dropped his cigarette without even realizing it. And later, when he saw Murphy holding me back, I'm sure he thought I was being mauled."

"Deirdre." Ronan put a fist beneath her chin, lifting her face. "This wasn't your fault, or mine, either. It was an accident."

She took a deep breath, nodding slowly. "I know."

When he took her hand and led her away, she let him. They crossed the yard and walked around to the back of the house, mounting the steps. But before she could reach for the doorknob, Ronan tugged on her hand.

"Let's sit for a minute."

She didn't want to "sit for a minute." Ronan had been the very image of a concerned spouse at the hospital. She'd had a sonogram done so they could be sure the baby hadn't been harmed, and he'd asked the technician at least two dozen questions. And at one point in her stay, one of the nurses told him he'd have to step out for a moment while they checked his wife.

The innocent mistake had cut into her heart, far deeper than the mild burns on the backs of her calves. No, she didn't want to be anywhere near Ronan. The less time she spent in his presence, the better. That way, she could get used to a life without him.

He tugged again, harder, and she realized she'd stopped in her tracks. "I really have to let Murphy out," she said.

"In a minute." He leaned against the porch railing and loosely clasped her wrists, holding her in front of him. "I've been misunderstanding you or you've been misunderstanding me since the first night we made love on this porch. It stops tonight. Remember I wanted to talk to you last evening when you got it into your head to take a little drive?"

She nodded, wondering what purpose this rehash could have. "I don't—"

"That's right," he said, putting his fingers against her lips. "You don't talk. I'm the one doing the talking. You're the one doing the listening. Now—" He set his hands at her waist and pulled her closer. "I asked you to marry me and you said no. There are a lot of reasons that marriage would be a good thing for you and me. I think I've already told you most of them."

She could feel her eyes filling with tears, and she started to turn away, but he held her easily in place. "But there's one reason I forgot, one that's the most important of all."

As his words registered, the first faint blossoms of hope began to unfurl within her. Slowly, afraid she was reading too much into his statement, she lifted her gaze to his. The warmth in the hazel depths made her swallow involuntarily.

Ronan reached for her hands again, holding them clasped between their bodies. "I love you, Deirdre. I should have said it weeks ago, but I was too stupid to understand it. Feeling like I'm only half-complete when I'm not with you is love. Wanting to find you to share good news when my editor calls and says she likes my outline is love. Lying awake staring at the ceiling because you aren't in my arms is love.'' He brought her hands to his lips, kissing the back of first one and then the other. ''Is that what was missing from my proposal the first time around?''

She didn't answer immediately; she couldn't. As he searched her brimming eyes, she saw a sudden, endearing uncertainty cloud his gaze.

''Is that what was missing?'' he repeated. ''If not, please tell me what you want from me, and I'll do it. I'll do anything if it means you'll agree to marry me and keep loving me for the rest of my life.''

Finally she found her voice. ''That's what was missing,'' she confirmed, joy spreading through her. ''I don't want anything but you, Ronan. I love you. Let's get married.''

He drew her against him, holding her closely all along his hard, hot body, running his hands over her as if he was relearning every curve. ''Name the day.''

But as he lowered his head to kiss her, they both heard the telephone inside the house shrilling. Ronan groaned, his mouth a breath above hers.

''Shall we ignore it?'' she whispered.

Slowly he set her away from him as the phone rang again. ''It might be the boys. Better get it.''

She quickly unlocked the back door and reached for the phone as Murphy bounded out into the yard.

After listening to the caller, grinning and answering when required, she stuck her head out the door. Ronan was rolling around on the porch with the dog, and her heart contracted. He was really going to be hers! Together they would raise their children in a warm, loving household, the kind she'd always dreamed of.

"It's my mother," she said, pausing until he looked up at her. "She says the boys put Jell-O in the pool because they wanted to make the water firm enough to walk on and can she please bring them home now?"

Epilogue

"Uh oh. Put on your bullet-proof vest." Ronan nudged Jack in the ribs, nodding toward the woman walking toward them from the picnic tables.

Jack looked in the same direction, eyeing Jillian Kerr's all-white, formfitting sundress. Her blond hair bounced around her neck as she came toward them, carrying Jack's daughter, Alexa. "Wonder what she's going to chew us out about now?" He shook his head. "Too bad that woman has a tougher hide than a crocodile and a bite to match. I've got about a million friends who have bounced off her armor."

"Not a bad comparison," said Ronan, subsiding as the crocodile came within earshot.

"Hi, fellas." Close up, Jillian looked less than immaculate. There was a smear of chocolate across her shoulder that matched the ring around Alexa's mouth, and the dusty footprint from a tiny shoe decorated the skirt of her white dress.

"Hey, Jill." Jack's best line of defense was definitely to attack first. "You're looking a little the worse for wear. Kids getting the best of you?"

"No, but I'll know better than to wear white around your midget again." Her tone was warm as she pressed a kiss to the tip of Alexa's nose. Then she heaved an exaggerated sigh and struck a pose. "It doesn't really matter, though. I look fabulous, no matter what I'm wearing."

"You flatter yourself," Jack shot back, clearly pleased with himself for getting in the last word.

But Jillian didn't take offense. "Somebody's got to," she said drolly. Then she turned to Ronan. "You know, Ronan, I have to give you credit." The pretty blond gave him the first genuine, uncomplicated smile of simple friendliness he'd seen since he'd met her.

"Gee, whiz." He mimed growing faint as he turned to Jack. "She's giving me credit. I don't think I can take it." In the nine months since he'd married Deirdre, he'd come to a sort of armed stand-off with Jillian, ignoring her unless circumstances absolutely forced them to acknowledge each other. The woman had the temperament of a viper and a tongue like a shrew.

Now she stood in front of him, still smiling, but there wasn't a trace of malice or sarcasm in her tone. "I could tell that you were mad enough to deck me the day Dee told us she was pregnant. I might even have been pushing a few of your buttons on purpose—"

"Might have been?"

"But you never seriously considered it."

"Oh, no?" He raised an eyebrow.

"You know what I mean," she said. "Deirdre needed a man who doesn't think violence is an acceptable way to solve a problem. I think I like you."

"Gee, I'm flattered." He wasn't ready to forgive her for some of those stinging comments yet. But her sunny smile was infectious, and after a moment he felt himself struggling not to smile back at her. Finally he grinned, shaking his head. "You're a smart aleck, and a pain in the butt. But I think I like you, too."

"Friends?" She stuck out her hand.

"Friends," he agreed. Over her head, his wife caught his eye, and the warmth in the unspoken message made him feel a little guilty. Though Deirdre had never said anything, he knew the animosity between her husband and her best friend had bothered her. As he drew away from the handshake, he noticed that Jillian's smile had grown distinctly smug. "Now what are you up to?" he demanded.

Jillian made her eyes round and innocent. "Who, me?" Then she turned to Jack. "You owe me a C-note."

Ronan was puzzled. "Why do you owe her a hundred bucks?" he said to the bigger man.

Jack was practically foaming at the mouth as he opened his wallet and extracted five twenties. He slapped them into Jillian's outstretched palm. "At your wedding, I bet her it would take at least a year before she could charm you into smiling at her."

"Thanks. To both of you," she said with a grin, before blowing them both a kiss and walking away trailing a laugh behind her.

"Oh. Sorry. I lasted nine months." Laughter bubbled up and rolled out before he could control it. "Maybe if you kiss her, ah, feet, she'll prorate it," he said, still chuckling.

"Fat chance." Jack slung an arm around Ronan's shoulders and caught him in a friendly headlock. "Deirdre looks great with a baby in her arms again, pal."

"She looks great, period." Ronan gave Jack a hefty shove that sent him staggering back a step. "Your boy isn't going to be allowed near my baby girl, if he's anything like you."

"Brooks is exactly like me." Jack lifted an arm and curled it, exaggerating the biceps. "And the next one's going to be, too."

"The next one's going to be a girl." Ronan glanced across the grass at Frannie, who had just announced she was expecting another little Ferris to arrive in December. She was leaning over Ronan's daughter Maureen, snuggled in Deirdre's arms. Maureen would be two months old next week, on the twentieth of May. His life had been changed forever the day a nurse had handed his newborn child to him. He'd looked into the tiny face and seen himself. He hadn't thought he could love Deirdre any more than he already did.

He'd been wrong. A warm, satisfied feeling swelled in his chest as he looked at his two women. His. And they both loved him.

Habit made him glance around for Lee and Tommy, but they were nowhere to be seen. Not a good omen. His sons could wreak havoc in a shorter amount of time than an earthquake. Out of sight was definitely not out of mind with them.

Deirdre rose from her chair as he started across the grass, and they met near the barbecue pit.

"Hey, handsome," she said. "Want to make a date for tonight?"

Her words made his pulse leap. Along with other parts of him. "Love to." He put his arms around her, the baby cuddled between them. "Six weeks away from you made me so horny it's going to take months to wear off."

She smiled, deliberately pressing herself closer so that their bodies were a seamless fit and her voice was a husky murmur. "Good."

And as he dropped his head and sought her lips, he felt the sweet warmth that her loving presence always offered him. It was so much more than simply sex, that he was humbled anew every time she turned those big green eyes his way. "Do you know what today is?" he muttered against her lips.

"A good day for making love?" She shifted her hips in

the tiniest motion, but it made him suck in his breath and groan.

"That, too." He caught her by the hips when she would have moved again. "Stop that, or we're going to give our friends the shock of their lives." He looked down at her, savoring the moment. "One year ago today I walked into a grocery store and found the woman of my dreams."

Her eyes widened, and the dimples he so loved appeared in her cheeks. "You're right!" Her smile was crafty. "I guess we'll have to figure out some way to celebrate on our date tonight."

He laughed. "You've got a one-track mind, woman." But he didn't care. He was counting the hours, too, until he could get her alone and show her just how much this anniversary meant to him. The day he'd walked into that supermarket was the luckiest day of his life. He'd found the part of himself he hadn't even realized was missing— the part that had allowed him to open his heart and fill it with a woman's gentle love. With Deirdre's love.

* * * * *

Watch for Jillian's story
in

THE BRIDE MEANS BUSINESS

the third book in Anne Marie Winston's
exciting series
BUTLER COUNTY BRIDES.

Coming this March from Silhouette Desire.

Here come the...

BUTLER COUNTY Brides

an exciting Desire miniseries by
Anne Marie Winston

Meet three small-town best friends who bring three of the sexiest, most powerful bachelors in Butler County to their knees...!

THE BABY CONSULTANT—January 1999
DEDICATED TO DEIRDRE—February 1999
THE BRIDE MEANS BUSINESS—March 1999

Three brides' tales of walking down the aisle are coming your way in 1999—only from Silhouette Desire!

Available wherever Silhouette books are sold.

FORTUNE'S Children™

*The Fortune family requests
the honor of your presence at the weddings of*

FORTUNE'S CHILDREN™

The Brides

Silhouette Desire's scintillating new miniseries,
featuring the beloved Fortune family
and five of your favorite authors.

The Honor Bound Groom—**January 1999**
by Jennifer Greene (SD #1190)

Society Bride—**February 1999**
by Elizabeth Bevarly (SD #1196)

And look for more **FORTUNE'S CHILDREN:
THE BRIDES** installments by Leanne Banks,
Susan Crosby and Merline Lovelace,
coming in spring 1999.

Available at your favorite retail outlet.

Silhouette®

SILHOUETTE® Desire®

COMING NEXT MONTH